Penguin Books

Utterly Trivial Knowledge: The Pop Game

Utterly Trivial Knowledge: The Pop Game

David Robins

Penguin Books

Penguin Books Ltd, Harmondsworth, Middlesex, England
Viking Penguin Inc., 40 West 23rd Street, New York, New York 10010, USA
Penguin Books Australia Ltd, Ringwood, Victoria, Australia
Penguin Books Canada Ltd, 2801 John Street, Markham, Ontario, Canada L3R 1B4
Penguin Books (NZ) Ltd, 182–190 Wairau Road, Auckland 10, New Zealand

First published 1987

Filmset in 9/10 Century by
Rowland Phototypesetting Ltd
Bury St Edmunds, Suffolk
Printed in Great Britain by
Cox and Wyman Ltd, Reading, Berks

Introduction

A word of explanation

Each of the 225 sets of questions in this book are divided into six sections, roughly corresponding to those set out below:

1. *The Name Game*. For example, by what name was John Simon Beverley better known?
2. *Golden Oldies*. For those who still remember what a Dansette is (or rather was).
3. *The Fabulous Sixties*. A section for devotees of dinosaur culture.
4. *Seventies and Eighties*. Pop and rock in the age of the short, sharp shock, unemployment and privatisation.
5. *Pop Luck*. A mixed bag of curious and wonderful facts.
6. *Rockscreen*. Films, musicals, TV: from Rick Nelson's screen triumph in *Rio Bravo* to Michael Jackson's burning problems on video.

This book is dedicated to:

Alfy, Barbara Ann, Bridget the Midget, Bungalow Bill; Carol, Caroline, Carrie Anne, Claudette and Clair; (Deni) Denise, Delilah, Diane, Diana and Dona; Eleanor Rigby, Elouise and Ernie; Frankie and Fernando; Gaye, Happy Jack, Sister Jane, Jumpin' Jack Flash, Jeannie and Jude; Ipanema (the girl from); the Ladies Jane, Madonna, D'Arbanville and Day; Laura (tell her I love her), Layla, Lola, Lucille, (be bop a) Lula, and Lulu (don't bring her); Mandy, Maria, Maybelline, Michelle, Maggie May, Mony Mony, and the Man from Laramie; Nancy, Nathan Jones and Norma Jean; Prudence, Puck, Queenie, Ramona and the Real Roxanne; Rosetta, Rupert and Ruby Tuesday; Sally (long tall) and Sally (pride of); Sheila, Sloopy, Snoopy, Speedy Gonzales, Samantha, Sarah, Susanne and Sylvia's mother; Tommy, Vincent, Willy the Pimp, Zorba, Zabadak, Davy Crockett, Champion the Wonder Horse, the son of Hickory Hollis, Abraham Martin and John, a boy named Su, and not forgetting – Peggy Sue!

Dave Robins

PS What about Rudolph the Red-nosed Reindeer? (ed.)

1

1. Who is David Jones better known as?
2. Who sang 'They call me the fat man cos I weigh 200 pounds'?
3. Which music did Sir Coxsone Dodd and Studio One pioneer?
4. Who toned down his act after a 14-year-old girl died at his London show in 1974?
5. According to Roger Miller, what 'swings like a pendulum do'?
6. Who directed *Fame*?

76

1. What was Elvis Presley's middle name?
2. How did Bobby Darin die?
3. What band's name is jumbled Latin meaning 'far from these things'?
4. Who packaged an eight-song cassette to resemble a Marlboro cigarette pack?
5. What is James Last's country of origin?
6. Which guest on *Desert Island Discs* chose *16 Tons*, *Rock Rock Rock*, and *Rule Britannia*?

151

1. Who named his daughter Tulip after his hit record *Tiptoe Through the Tulips* in 1968?
2. Who wrote *Rock a Beatin' Boogie*?
3. Who had one hit, *Something in the Air*, and then disbanded?
4. Who sings about 'highways jammed with broken heroes on a last-chance power drive'?
5. Who devised and introduced *Opportunity Knocks*?
6. Which band is named after a character from the movie *Barbarella*?

1

1. David Bowie.
2. Fats Domino.
3. Reggae.
4. David Cassidy.
5. England.
6. Alan Parker Jnr.

76

1. Aaron.
2. Heart attack (during subsequent open heart surgery).
3. Procol Harum.
4. Malcolm McLaren.
5. West Germany.
6. Princess Margaret.

151

1. Tiny Tim.
2. Bill Haley.
3. Thunderclap Newman.
4. Bruce Springsteen.
5. Hughie Green.
6. Duran Duran.

2

1. Who is 'Tiger Tom of Pontypridd'?
2. Who was the first rock singer to double-track his voice and guitar?
3. Who produced all the Beatles' albums?
4. What form of black dance music came to prominence through a chart hit of The Sugarhill Gang?
5. Who is the only knight to have gone to no. 1 in the charts?
6. Who once co-starred with Petula Clark in a musical version of *Goodbye Mr Chips*?

77

1. Which Irish chanteuse began life as Rosemary Brown?
2. What group had smashes with *Only You* and *The Great Pretender*?
3. Who was the lead singer in the group Them?
4. Who debuted with the single *Planet Earth* in 1981 and were described as 'New Romantics'?
5. Which country singer became Governor of Louisiana?
6. Who starred in television's *McKenzie* and *Three of a Kind*?

152

1. Who was 'King of the Twist'?
2. Who made his mark on American rock and roll with *Reet Petite*?
3. What is Van Morrison's home town?
4. Who covered *Wherever I Lay My Hat That's My Home* and was hailed as the best white soul voice in Britain?
5. Which jazz band played at Buck House at the wedding of Charles and Diana?
6. Who played Jesus in *Godspell* in 1971?

2

1. Tom Jones.
2. Buddy Holly.
3. George Martin.
4. Rap (The record was *Rapper's Delight*).
5. Harry Secombe (*This is My Song*, 1967).
6. Peter O'Toole.

77

1. Dana.
2. The Platters.
3. Van Morrison.
4. Duran Duran.
5. Jimmie Davis.
6. Tracy Ullman.

152

1. Chubby Checker.
2. Jackie Wilson.
3. Belfast.
4. Paul Young.
5. Kenny Ball jazz band.
6. David Essex.

3

1. What is the title of Adam Faith's autobiography?
2. Where is 'the tiny house by the tiny sea'?
3. Which folk-rock band's signature tune was *Fog on the Tyne*?
4. Whose version of *Rivers of Babylon* is the third biggest-selling UK single of all time?
5. What part of the anatomy is Chuck Berry referring to in *My Ding-a-Ling*?
6. What musical is based on Bernard Shaw's *Pygmalion*?

78

1. Who was known as 'The Old Groaner'?
2. Jerry Keller had his one-and-only UK no. 1 in 1969 with which classic teen ballad?
3. Who heard the sound of *Distant Drums*?
4. Whose album *Bat Out of Hell* remained in the UK album charts for six years?
5. Who wrote *I Wanna Be Your Man*?
6. What Cole Porter musical includes *C'est Magnifique*, *I Love Paris*, and *It's All Right With Me*?

153

1. Who was referred to as 'The Metal Guru'?
2. Which gravel-voiced cockney had a hit with a rock version of *Ain't Misbehavin'*?
3. In Shirley Ellis's *The Clapping Song* (1965), where did the monkey chew tobacco?
4. Which rock star organized ARMS, a charity to combat multiple sclerosis?
5. What city does Frank Sinatra call 'My kind of town'?
6. What musical includes the song *I Don't Know How to Love Him*?

3

1. *Poor Me.*
2. 'In Gilliegillieotsenfeffercatsenelerbogen by the sea.'
3. Lindisfarne.
4. Boney M.
5. The penis.
6. *My Fair Lady.*

78

1. Bing Crosby.
2. *Here Comes Summer.*
3. Jim Reeves.
4. Meat Loaf.
5. Lennon and McCartney.
6. *Can Can.*

153

1. Marc Bolan.
2. Tommy Bruce.
3. On the street-car line.
4. Ronnie Lane.
5. Chicago.
6. *Jesus Christ Superstar.*

4

1. Who said, 'On stage I make love to 25,000 people. Then I go home alone'?
2. Who was the other half of Pearl Carr?
3. 'People try to put us d-down'. Next line?
4. What band was fronted by Willy de Ville?
5. Who was left-handed, used right-hand-model guitars, and played them upside down?
6. Who sang *Mrs Robinson* in the movie *The Graduate*?

79

1. Who was once a chicken-plucker called Ernest Evans?
2. What hit instrumental of 1962 was inspired by the launch of a communications satellite?
3. Who was the most successful female solo singer in the UK sixties singles charts?
4. Who had a major hit single in 1978 with *Lay Down Sally*?
5. Who 'walked like a woman and talked like a man'?
6. Who entered pop music by sending it up in the film *Idle on Parade*?

154

1. Who were 'The Tottenham Sound'?
2. Who went to no. 1 in the UK in 1955 with *Stranger in Paradise*?
3. Who sang, 'people look strange when you're a stranger, faces look ugly when you're alone'?
4. Who had a hit with *Every 1's a Winner*?
5. Which former rock star became an editor at Fabers?
6. Which rock star appeared as a virgin soldier in the movie *Virgin Soldiers*?

4

1. Janis Joplin.
2. Teddy Johnson.
3. 'Just because we g-get around'.
4. Mink de Ville.
5. Jimi Hendrix.
6. Simon and Garfunkel.

79

1. Chubby Checker.
2. *Telstar* (by the Tornados).
3. Brenda Lee.
4. Eric Clapton.
5. *Lola* (by the Kinks).
6. Anthony Newley.

154

1. The Dave Clark 5.
2. Tony Bennett.
3. The Doors.
4. Hot Chocolate.
5. Pete Townshend.
6. David Bowie.

5

1. Who stood five feet seven inches in his high-heeled boots and was nicknamed Rock's answer to Howard Hughes?
2. 'She's my baby . . . and I don't mean maybe'. Who was Gene Vincent referring to?
3. Who wrote the Searchers' hit *Needles and Pins*?
4. What did Vikki Watson win in 1985?
5. Which song has the line, 'Think of all the hate there is in Red China'?
6. On the TV spectacular *One World*, what did the Beatles play to 400 million people?

80

1. Which trad jazzer's trademark is a bowler hat and waistcoat?
2. 'Kiss me, honey honey, kiss me'. What is the next line?
3. Who walked off stage in the middle of a Madison Square Garden Peace Benefit Concert in 1970?
4. Mikey Craig and drummer Jon Moss became famous with which group?
5. How does The Shangri-Las' *Leader of the Pack* dance?
6. Who gave Alec Guinness his first screen kiss, in *The Card*?

155

1. What is Georgie Fame's signature tune?
2. What was Marvin Rainwater's chart-topper of 1958?
3. Who composed The Stones' hit *I Just Wanna Make Love to You*?
4. Who wrote *Rock On*?
5. Which former record producer became Prime Minister of Jamaica?
6. Who co-wrote and starred in *The Roar of the Greasepaint, the Smell of the Crowd*?

5

1. Phil Spector.
2. Be-Bop-A-Lula.
3. Jackie De Shannon.
4. The Eurovision Song Contest.
5. *Eve of Destruction* (by Barry McGuire).
6. *All You Need is Love*.

80

1. Acker Bilk.
2. 'Thrill me, honey honey, thrill me'.
3. Jimi Hendrix.
4. Culture club.
5. 'Close, very close'.
6. Petula Clark.

155

1. *Yeh, Yeh*.
2. *A Whole Lotta Woman*.
3. Muddy Waters.
4. David Essex.
5. Edward Seaga.
6. Anthony Newley.

6

1. Who were once a 16-year-old duo called Tom and Jerry?
2. Can anything stop the Duke of Earl?
3. What kind of wedding did Roy C. invite us to in 1966?
4. *Follow the Leaders* was the first hit for which band in 1981?
5. Which P.M.'s speeches got to no. 6 in the charts in 1965?
6. Keith Carradine's *I'm Easy* won a musical Oscar in 1975 for which movie?

81

1. Which pop composer's brother is a professional cellist?
2. Who created a record in 1955 with five hits in the top 20 at the same time?
3. Who had hits with *Be My Baby* and *Baby I Love You*?
4. What punk band released a single called *Boredom*?
5. What London street is nicknamed Tin Pan Alley?
6. Who both starred in and sang the theme from *Dr Kildare*?

156

1. Whose name is synonymous with the jazz violin?
2. What comic trad jazz band featured Whispering Paul McDowell?
3. Who topped the charts in 1965 with *I Got You Babe*?
4. Who released an album entitled *Masterblaster* in 1980?
5. Who wrote *Send in the Clowns*?
6. Who wrote the score for the film *Willie Wonka and the Chocolate Factory*, including the song *Candy Man*?

6

1. Simon and Garfunkel.
2. No, 'Nothing can stop the Duke of Earl'.
3. *Shotgun Wedding*.
4. Killing Joke.
5. Sir Winston Churchill (*The Wartime Speeches*).
6. *Nashville*.

81

1. Andrew Lloyd Webber.
2. Ruby Murray.
3. The Ronettes.
4. The Buzzcocks.
5. Denmark Street.
6. Richard Chamberlain.

156

1. Stephane Grappelli.
2. The Temperance Seven.
3. Sonny and Cher.
4. Stevie Wonder.
5. Stephen Sondheim.
6. Anthony Newley.

7

1. Which country star got her name from a hamburger stand?
2. How does King Creole hold his guitar?
3. Which band performed an anthem in homage to heroin?
4. On what album does Van Morrison advise us to 'Listen to the Lion'?
5. Who wrote and performed a hit song about his manager's newly born daughter Clare?
6. Who played Lulu in the 1984 National Theatre production of *Guys and Dolls*?

82

1. Which rocker is nicknamed 'The Killer'?
2. Who was the first Brit to top the US charts, with *He's Got the Whole World in His Hands*?
3. How many Temptations were there?
4. Who pushed the Prince Charming look?
5. Where is Motown?
6. Who had a hit with the theme song from the movie *Ghostbusters*?

157

1. What is Elvis Costello's real name?
2. What was Roy Orbison's trademark?
3. Who had a hit in 1965 with *Here Comes the Night*?
4. Who won the Ivor Novello songwriter of the year award in 1985?
5. Who proclaimed, 'Thatcher is the first great leader since Churchill'?
6. Who recorded the theme for the Bond movie *A View to a Kill*?

7

1. Crystal Gayle.
2. Like a tommy gun.
3. Velvet Underground.
4. *St Dominic's Preview*.
5. Gilbert O'Sullivan.
6. Lulu.

82

1. Jerry Lee Lewis.
2. Laurie London.
3. Five.
4. Adam Ant.
5. Detroit.
6. Ray Parker Jnr.

157

1. Declan Aloysius McManus.
2. Dark glasses.
3. Them.
4. George Michael.
5. Gary Numan.
6. Duran Duran.

8

1. Who pleaded for an international holiday in remembrance of Martin Luther King?
2. Who is remembered for his comedy hits, *Hole in the Ground* and *Right said Fred*?
3. Who had a US no. 1 in 1968 with *Harper Valley PTA*?
4. Who were described by Nik Cohn as 'The poets of suburban angst'?
5. What Rogers and Hart standard does Lionel Bart's *Fings Ain't What They Used to Be* sound remarkably like?
6. In which movie does Elvis sing in German?

83

1. Three artists surnamed Preston had UK hits in the sixties. Can you name them?
2. Who sang *Honky Tonk Man*, which became a hit after his death?
3. The Radha Krishna Temple made no. 12 in the charts in 1969 with what?
4. Who went to the top with *Long-haired Lover from Liverpool* in 1972?
5. Who once played a massive sellout concert at the Valley, former home of Charlton Athletic FC?
6. Who duetted 'I give to you as you give to me, true love' in the film *High Society*?

158

1. Who were Dias, Fagen, Hodder, Becker and Baxter known as?
2. What kind of doll did Perry Como sing about in 1958?
3. Who had eleven consecutive no. 1 singles from 1963 to 1966?
4. Who toured both the USA and the USSR in 1986?
5. Who was the rock star whose interest in the black arts prompted him to buy an occult bookstore?
6. What musical includes the song *Hernando's Hideaway*?

8

1. Stevie Wonder.
2. Bernard Cribbins.
3. Jeannie C. Riley.
4. Simon and Garfunkel.
5. *Mountain Greenery.*
6. *GI Blues.*

83

1. Johnny, Mike and Billy.
2. Johnny Horton.
3. *Hare Krishna Mantra.*
4. Little Jimmy Osmond.
5. The Who.
6. Bing Crosby and Grace Kelly.

158

1. Steely Dan.
2. Kewpie Doll.
3. The Beatles.
4. UB40.
5. Jimmy Page (of Led Zeppelin).
6. *The Pyjama Game.*

9

1. Who married Miss Vicky on 17 December 1969?
2. In Eddie Cochran's *Three Steps to Heaven*, what is Step One?
3. Whose psychedelic Rolls Royce was sold for 2 million dollars in 1985?
4. Who was the driving force behind Derek and the Dominoes?
5. Which French pop star married Johnny Halliday?
6. What do Hunter Davies, Philip Norman and Anthony Scaduto have in common?

84

1. Who was Tina Turner's husband and stage-partner?
2. What was Chuck Berry's first hit?
3. Who covered Major Lance's 1963 hit *um-um-um-um-um-um* in Britain?
4. Which punk band was fronted by Jimmy Pursey?
5. What does RAR stand for?
6. Who had the biggest-selling rock video of all time with *Thriller*?

159

1. Which rock star's father was chief sports-writer for the *Toronto Globe & Mail*?
2. Why did February make Don McClean shiver in *American Pie*?
3. Who was *The Times* editor who supported the Stones on trial in an editorial entitled 'Why Break a Butterfly on a Wheel'?
4. What style of music is associated with the group 14 Carat Soul?
5. According to Malcolm McLaren where does the first Buffalo Gal go?
6. Which rock magazine was founded by Jann Wenner?

9

1. Tiny Tim.
2. 'You find someone to love'.
3. John Lennon.
4. Eric Clapton.
5. Silvie Vartan.
6. They have all written books about the Beatles.

84

1. Ike.
2. *Maybelline*.
3. Wayne Fontana.
4. Sham 69.
5. Rock Against Racism.
6. Michael Jackson.

159

1. Neil Young.
2. It was the month Buddy Holly died.
3. William Rees Mogg.
4. A cappella.
5. Round the outside.
6. *Rolling Stone*.

10

1. Who was born Cherilyn Sarkasian LaPier?
2. In *Fings Ain't What They Used to Be*, what have they turned the local pally into?
3. Who topped the US charts in 1963 with *It's My Party*?
4. Who in 1976 recorded a 13-song album, including *Now I want to Sniff Some Glue*, lasting under half an hour?
5. Who wrote *Solitaire*, *Stairway to Heaven*, and *That's Where the Music Takes me*?
6. Whose last musical show was *Gay's The Word*, in 1951?

35

1. What 'King of showbiz' is one-eyed, black and Jewish?
2. Which modern jazzer had a pop success in 1961 with *Take 5*?
3. Who composed the Rolling Stones' *Time is on My Side*?
4. Who said to Duran Duran fans: 'You need serious help because these people are conning you'?
5. Which DJ formed his own record label, Dandelion?
6. What manufactured Teen Idol appeared with John Wayne in *North to Alaska*?

160

1. Who is Harry Edward Nelson III better known as?
2. What will 'I bring again when it's spring again'?
3. On Bob Dylan's *Maggie's Farm*, who is outside guarding the door?
4. Whose multi-million Christmas hit contained the message 'war is over'?
5. 'I shot the sheriff'. But who didn't I shoot?
6. Who starred in a TV production of Brecht's *Baal* in 1982?

10

1. Cher.
2. A bowling alley.
3. Leslie Gore.
4. The Ramones.
5. Neil Sedaka.
6. Ivor Novello.

85

1. Sammy Davis Jnr.
2. Dave Brubeck.
3. Jerry Ragavoy.
4. John Lydon.
5. John Peel.
6. Fabian.

160

1. Nilsson.
2. 'Tulips from Amsterdam'.
3. The National Guard.
4. John Lennon and Yoko Ono.
5. 'I didn't shoot no deputy'.
6. David Bowie.

11

. Who lost his two sons in a fire and his wife in a bike crash?
. What did Jim Reeves want his girl to put her sweet lips a little closer to?
. Who was with The Beachcombers before joining The Who?
What does ABBA stand for?
. In Bob Dylan's *Desolation Row*, what colour are they painting the passports?
. Which former sixties chart-topper produced a West End musical starring Cliff Richard and (sort of) Laurence Olivier?

36

. Who postponed marriage to a Bee Gee in 1969 to take part in the Eurovision Song Contest?
. Who released a string of gunfighter ballads and western songs starting with *El Paso* in 1959?
. Who dreamed about a knight in armour saying something about a queen?
. The Knopflers are the brains behind which group?
. Which folkie wrote a song about heroin entitled *Needle of Death*?
. Who wrote a book called *Spaniard in the Works*?

161

. Who is Sing along a Max?
. Who wrote *Shake, Rattle and Roll*?
. Which Doors single made no. 1 in the US charts?
. Which eighties pop star was a double-glazing salesman from Ipswich?
. What do Siouxsie, David Bowie, and Billy Idol all have in common?
. Duane Eddy had a hit in Britain with the theme from which TV series?

11

1. Roy Orbison.
2. The phone (*He'll Have to Go*).
3. Keith Moon.
4. Anna, Bjorn, Benni and Anni.
5. Brown.
6. Dave Clark.

86

1. Lulu.
2. Marty Robbins.
3. Neil Young (on the album *After the Goldrush*).
4. Dire Straits.
5. Bert Jansch.
6. John Lennon.

161

1. Max Bygraves.
2. Big Joe Turner.
3. *Light My Fire*.
4. Nik Kershaw.
5. They all come from Bromley.
6. *Peter Gunn*.

12

1. Who is 'Mr Tubular Bells'?
2. Why was Jerry Lee Lewis booed off the stage of the Kilburn Gaumont in 1958?
3. What instrument did Ravi Shankar make popular in the sixties?
4. Who won the Eurovision Song Contest in 1976 with *Save Your Kisses for Me*?
5. Who was the first to use strings on a rock and roll record?
6. Who played Maria in a stage revival of *The Sound of Music* in 1981?

87

1. What is producer George Morton's nickname?
2. Who had a million-seller in France with *Viens danser le twist* in 1961?
3. Which band tried to cash in on their association with the Beatles with an album called *Saga of the Beatles*?
4. Green is a key member of which eighties group?
5. What is Tamla Motown's country label?
6. Who fronts a regular BBC radio programme called *A King in New York*?

162

1. What was Tommy Steele's job before he became a pop star in 1956?
2. Who got her big break baby-sitting for songwriters King and Goffin?
3. What veteran band, started at school, performed in 1966 as The Spectators touring holiday camps?
4. Who are OMD?
5. Who made a study of Dylan's garbage?
6. Who changed his name to Christie after seeing the film *Darling*?

12

1. Mike Oldfield.
2. Because he had married his 13-year-old cousin.
3. The sitar.
4. Brotherhood of Man.
5. Buddy Holly.
6. Petula Clark.

87

1. Shadow.
2. Johnny Halliday.
3. Johnny and the Hurricanes.
4. Scritti Politti.
5. Hitsville.
6. Jonathan King.

162

1. Merchant Seaman.
2. Little Eva.
3. Status Quo.
4. Orchestral Manoeuvres in the Dark.
5. A. J. Weberman.
6. Tony Christie.

3

Who started life as Gerry Dorsey?

Which chart success for Rosemary Clooney became a hit in the seventies for Shakin' Stevens?

Which Motown band exhorted *Reach Out*?

Who is the voice behind 'Just One Cornetto'?

Who had her first radio series at the age of 9 and won a US Grammy award with *I Know a Place*?

Who won an award for best film soundtrack, for the epic *Flash Gordon*?

38

What is Frankie Vaughan's signature tune?

Who played bass for the Silver Beatles in 1959?

Which band included Chas Chandler, Eric Burdon, and Alan Price?

Who became the first woman to win the Ivor Novello songwriting award with *Won't Somebody Dance With Me*, in 1974?

Who announced 'The Ten Commandments of Man as Given to Woman'?

Who teamed up with half of Abba to write the musical *Chess*?

163

What was Sid Vicious's real name?

Who did Bing Crosby go fishin' with?

Who had the best-selling British single of 1965 with *I'll Never Find Another You*?

Who duetted with Elton John on *Don't Go Breakin' My Heart* in 1976?

Who signed for Brentford FC before becoming a rock star?

Who plays an Eddie Cochran-worshipping garage mechanic in the film *Radio On*?

13

1. Engelbert Humperdinck.
2. *This Ole House.*
3. The Four Tops.
4. Nick Curtis.
5. Petula Clark.
6. Queen.

88

1. *Gimme the Moonlight.*
2. Stuart Sutcliffe.
3. The Animals.
4. Lynsey De Paul.
5. Prince Buster.
6. Tim Rice.

163

1. John Simon Beverley.
2. Louis Armstrong (*Gone Fishing*).
3. The Seekers.
4. Kiki Dee.
5. Rod Stewart.
6. Sting.

4

Who is Neasden's 'Queen of Soul'?
How many Satins were there?
Who claimed that the Beatles were more popular than Jesus?
Who topped the UK pops with *Part of the Union*?
Who described meeting Chagall as 'a greater thrill than meeting Chuck Berry'?
Which band featured in the movie *Stop Making Sense*?

9

Who is five foot nothing, weighs a hundred and plenty and favours blonde wigs?
In *Summertime Blues*, why can't Eddie Cochran use his father's car?
Who did the Shangri-Las meet in the candy store?
Which soul dynasty includes brothers Bobby and Cecil, wife Linda, and Mother Naomi?
Who married Julianne Phillips in Oregon in 1985?
Which country was the setting for the movie *The Harder They Come*?

64

Who did Wayne County become?
Which country pop star once played baseball for the St Louis Cardinals?
Lamont, Eddie, and Brian were a songwriting team better known as – ?
Name the first Spanish singer to top the UK charts.
How many albums do you have to sell to go platinum?
In which movie does Elvis play a boxer?

14

1. Marie Wilson.
2. Five.
3. John Lennon.
4. The Strawbs.
5. Bill Wyman.
6. Talking Heads.

89

1. Dolly Parton.
2. 'Cos he didn't work late'.
3. *The Leader of the Pack.*
4. The Womacks.
5. Bruce Springsteen.
6. Jamaica.

164

1. Jane County.
2. Jim Reeves.
3. Holland, Dozier, Holland.
4. Julio Iglesias.
5. A million.
6. *Kid Galahad.*

15

1. Which British chanteuse was born in Tiger Bay, Cardiff?
2. Which song was a posthumous hit for Buddy Holly?
3. Who was the first English rock group to have a female drummer?
4. Charles Aznavour had his first British no. 1 in 1974 with which song?
5. On which Jamaican dance rhythm was Bluebeat based?
6. Who sang the theme from *Rawhide*?

90

1. Who called himself 'The Thin White Duke'?
2. Platters, Coasters, Diamonds and Drifters were all known for which sound?
3. Who sold most records in Britain in 1965 – the Beatles, Cliff Richard, the Stones, or the Seekers?
4. Who recorded a country album called *Daddy Was a Railroad Man*?
5. How many records are you allowed to choose on *Desert Island Discs*?
6. Who was spotted by Twiggy on *Opportunity Knocks* and signed up by Paul McCartney?

165

1. Who had an American chart-topper with *The Battle of New Orleans* and was known as the 'Singing Fisherman'?
2. 'So sad to watch good love go bad' was a line written by whom?
3. Who organized a 'sleep-in for peace' in Amsterdam?
4. Who first hit the heights with *Wuthering Heights*?
5. What is the Jamaican term for a DJ who ad libs over instrumental tracks?
6. Who was the female co-star with Cliff Richard in *Summer Holiday*?

15

1. Shirley Bassey.
2. *It Doesn't Matter Any More.*
3. The Honeycombs.
4. *She.*
5. Ska.
6. Frankie Laine.

90

1. David Bowie.
2. Doo-wop.
3. The Seekers.
4. Boxcar Willie.
5. Eight.
6. Mary Hopkin.

165

1. Johnny Horton.
2. The Everly Brothers.
3. John Lennon and Yoko Ono.
4. Kate Bush.
5. Toaster.
6. Susan Hampshire.

16

1. Who has been described as 'Tackie Mackie'?
2. Who was just walkin' in the rain in 1956?
3. *You're Driving Me Crazy* and *Pasadena* were big hits in 1962 for who?
4. What moved out of the Bronx to become 'The only clearly identifiable international youth style of the eighties'?
5. Which recording site near Birmingham, Alabama, has been popularized by leading black soul artists?
6. Who had her biggest hit with the song from a film about a massacre of Indians called *Soldier Blue*?

91

1. Which comedy duo's signature tune was *Goodbye*?
2. Whose signature tune was an instrumental version of *Zambesi*?
3. What did John Lennon change his middle name to after marrying Yoko?
4. Who topped the charts with *Mama Weer Al Crazee Now*?
5. 'What do you want to make those eyes at me for'. Next line?
6. Who co-starred with Phil Daniels in the film *Breaking Glass*?

166

1. Who dedicated his solo album to his cat (and they should have called the RSPCA)?
2. Who went to no. 4 in the UK with *Don't You Rock Me Daddy-O* in 1957?
3. According to Del Shannon, how many kinds of teardrop are there?
4. Who fronts the Waves?
5. Which rock luminary was arrested on an anti-apartheid demo in Washington in 1985?
6. Which tone-deaf TV pesonality put in a bid for worst-ever record with *Shifting Whispering Sands* in 1956?

16

1. Malcolm McLaren.
2. Johnny Ray.
3. The Temperance Seven.
4. Hip-hop.
5. Muscle Shoals.
6. Buffy Saint Marie.

91

1. Peter Cook and Dudley Moore.
2. Eddie Calvert.
3. Ono.
4. Slade.
5. 'If they don't mean what they say'.
6. Hazel O'Connor.

166

1. Freddie Mercury.
2. Lonnie Donegan.
3. Two.
4. Katrina.
5. Stevie Wonder.
6. Eamonn Andrews.

17

1. Who were originally called The Nightlife Thugs?
2. Who toured the UK with a Christian entertainment show called *Come Together*?
3. Who topped the pops with an instrumental entitled *Stranger on the Shore*?
4. Who became a preacher after hot oil was poured on him in the bath by a former girlfriend who then shot herself?
5. Who teamed up with jazz bassist Charlie Mingus just before his death?
6. Who played a hundred-year-old man in *The Hunger*?

92

1. Who presented *Desert Island Discs* until his death in 1985?
2. In the song by Johnny Preston, who was Running Bear's true love?
3. Which sixties classic by Creedence Clearwater Revival warns 'Look like we're in for nasty weather'?
4. Who wrote *Spasticus Autisticus* for the UN Year of the Disabled but it was rejected?
5. What is the rasta term for reggae?
6. In The Who's rock opera, what is the name of Tommy's wicked uncle?

167

1. Whose parents were called Gladys and Vernon?
2. Whose biggest hit was *Be-Bop-A-Lula*?
3. Who wanted to be *Bobby's Girl*?
4. Who went to no. 1 in 1986 with *Don't Leave Me This Way*?
5. What do Paul Kossoff, John Belushi, Tim Buckley, Phil Lynott, Keith Moon, and Jimi Hendrix all have in common?
6. Windsor Davies and Don Estelle of *It Aint Half 'ot Mum* went to the top in 1975 with which camp tune?

17

1. Boomtown Rats.
2. Pat Boone.
3. Acker Bilk.
4. Al Green.
5. Joni Mitchell.
6. David Bowie.

92

1. Roy Plomley.
2. Little White Dove.
3. *Bad Moon Rising*.
4. Ian Dury.
5. Rockers.
6. Ernie.

167

1. Elvis Presley.
2. Gene Vincent.
3. Susan Maughan.
4. The Communards.
5. They died of heroin overdoses.
6. *Whispering Grass*.

18

1. Which rapper's real name is Joseph Saddler?
2. How many were there in Lord Rockingham's band?
3. Who wrote the song *It's Good News Week*?
4. Whose record *The Breaks* popularized rap outside New York City?
5. Which DJ called his audience 'guys and gals'?
6. Which musical includes the songs *Sunrise Sunset* and *If I Were a Rich Man*?

93

1. Who is 'The world's most famous left-handed bassist'?
2. Which Tex-Mex singer was sentenced to five years in Louisiana for drug possession in 1960?
3. Who had hits with *Call Up the Groups* and *Pop go the Workers*?
4. Who is the half-Nigerian singer who favours backless evening dresses?
5. Who recorded an album live in Folsom prison?
6. Which Stones song was inspired by a novel by Bulgakov featuring a smooth-talking Satan?

168

1. Whose biography is entitled *Rocky Mountain Wonderboy*?
2. Who created the black leather image for Gene Vincent?
3. Where did Jim Morrison die of a heroin overdose?
4. Whose songs include *Some Candy Talking*, *Psychocandy*, and *Taste of Cindy*?
5. Who excused himself from performing in Live Aid by claiming it was a Jehovah's Witness holiday?
6. Which soul veteran starred in *Mad Max III*?

18

1. Grandmaster Flash.
2. Eleven.
3. Jonathan King.
4. Kurtis Blow.
5. Jimmy Savile.
6. *Fiddler on the Roof.*

93

1. Paul McCartney.
2. Freddie Fender.
3. The Barron Knights.
4. Sade.
5. Johnny Cash.
6. *Sympathy for the Devil.*

168

1. John Denver.
2. Jack Good.
3. Paris.
4. The Jesus and Mary Chain.
5. Michael Jackson.
6. Tina Turner.

19

1. Who was born Eugene Craddock in 1935?
2. Who had hits with *Beatnik Fly*, *Red River Rock* and *Crossfire*?
3. Which record label was founded by Berry Gordy?
4. Who stayed in the *Hotel California* in 1976?
5. Who said 'I don't know anything about music. In my line you don't have to'?
6. Which movie was based on Janis Joplin's life and starred Bette Midler?

94

1. Whose trademark is a single white glove?
2. 'Every night I hope and pray,' sang Bobby Darin. What for?
3. In which song did Barry Mcguire protest that 'even the Jordan River is goddamn exploding'?
4. Which band was renamed the Faces?
5. Which London rock promoter masterminded the Geldof Live Aid show in 1985?
6. Which folksinger wrote a novel entitled *Beautiful Losers*?

169

1. Which British R & B singer owed his name to his height of six feet seven inches?
2. Who composed *The Battle of New Orleans*?
3. Who turned down UN Secretary General Waldheim's plea to get back together to play a concert for the Vietnamese boat-people?
4. What was Derek and the Dominoes' greatest hit?
5. Where did the Wombles come from?
6. Which band starred in the movie *Rockers*?

19

1. Gene Vincent.
2. Johnny and the Hurricanes.
3. Motown Records.
4. The Eagles.
5. Elvis Presley.
6. *The Rose.*

94

1. Michael Jackson.
2. A dream lover.
3. *Eve of Destruction.*
4. The Small Faces.
5. Harvey Goldsmith.
6. Leonard Cohen.

169

1. Long John Baldry.
2. Jimmy Driftwood.
3. The Beatles.
4. *Layla.*
5. Wimbledon.
6. Burning Spear.

20

1. Who left as his legacy the line 'Oh baby that's what I like'?
2. Who duetted with Dinah Washington on the hit version of *You've Got What it Takes*?
3. Who topped the UK and US charts with *Locomotion*?
4. Which band was named after their manager stuck a pin in a US map and came up with a city in Michigan?
5. What is the term for African nightclub dance music influenced by calypso?
6. Who directed *A Hard Day's Night*?

95

1. Who was born in St Kitts, West Indies, in 1950 but grew up in Birmingham?
2. Who topped the UK charts in 1950 with *Only the Lonely*?
3. Which imaginary band based on a comic strip had a hit with *Sugar Sugar* in 1969?
4. Who was the brains behind the Sex Pistols?
5. What sound do headbangers listen to?
6. Which reggae movie was based on the true story of an outlaw called Rhygin?

170

1. Which eighties megastar has a minder called 'Big Chick'?
2. Who had a hit in Britain with a cover version of the US hit *The Battle of New Orleans*?
3. Which American band was the first to play in Czechoslovakia in 1968 before the arrival of Soviet tanks?
4. Who left the Moody Blues to join Wings?
5. Who leads his orchestra wearing tights, cape, gold chains on his bare chest, and dark glasses fronting a shaved head?
6. Which group is seen performing in a bar in *The French Connection*?

20

1. The Big Bopper.
2. Brook Benton.
3. Little Eva.
4. Bay City Rollers.
5. High Life.
6. Richard Lester.

95

1. Joan Armatrading.
2. Conway Twitty.
3. The Archies.
4. Malcolm McLaren.
5. Heavy Metal.
6. *The Harder They Come.*

170

1. Prince.
2. Lonnie Donegan.
3. The Beach Boys.
4. Denny Laine.
5. Isaac Hayes.
6. The Three Degrees.

21

1. Micky Dolenz, Mike Nesmith, Davy Jones and Peter Tork are better known as what?
2. Which bandleader and arranger was involved with Sinatra's greatest hits?
3. *Release Me*, *There Goes My Everything*, and *The Last Waltz* were smash hits for who?
4. Which resentful punk read English Literature at Sussex University?
5. Who owns a motel chain named after his million-seller, *King of the Road*?
6. Who published an autobiography entitled *Daybreak* in 1968?

96

1. Who was known as 'The King of Ameriachi'?
2. Name Johnny Parise's hit band?
3. Who was lead singer of Creedence Clearwater Revival?
4. Who was the first British pop star to perform in the Soviet Union?
5. How did Otis Redding die?
6. Who played Billy Holiday in *Lady Sings the Blues*?

171

1. Who was 'The Pelvis'?
2. Who wrote *The Book of Love*?
3. Who played harmonica accompaniment on *My Boy Lollipop*?
4. Jones, Cook and Matlock were part of which band?
5. Esther and Abi Ofarim were the first Israelis to top the UK charts with what?
6. Who was the first journalist to feature the Beatles in a national newspaper?

21

1. The Monkees.
2. Nelson Riddle.
3. Engelbert Humperdinck.
4. Billy Idol.
5. Roger Miller.
6. Joan Baez.

96

1. Herb Alpert.
2. Johnny and the Hurricanes.
3. John Fogerty.
4. Elton John.
5. In a plane crash.
6. Diana Ross.

171

1. Elvis Presley.
2. Davis, Patrick, and Malone.
3. Rod Stewart.
4. The Sex Pistols.
5. *Cindarella Rockafella.*
6. Maureen Cleave.

22

1. Who is known as His Royal Badness?
2. Who was killed in a car crash in Wiltshire in 1960?
3. Who preceded Ringo Starr on the drums in the Beatles?
4. Who played the Pinball Wizard in the movie version of *Tommy*?
5. What is the name for unaccompanied doo-wop harmonizing?
6. Who starred in the movie *Summer Holiday*?

97

1. What was John Lennon's middle name (before he changed it)?
2. Whose signature tune is *Whole Lotta Shakin'*?
3. Who was the brain behind the Mothers of Invention?
4. E.B.T.G. are the initials for which eighties group?
5. Which DJ refers to his listeners as pop-pickers?
6. Who always wore a denim cap and a harmonica harness on *Ready, Steady, Go*?

172

1. Which country pop star was known as Gentleman Jim?
2. 'I'm walkin' in the rain,' sang Del Shannon. To where?
3. What was Sandy Shaw's stage gimmick?
4. Name the cousin of Dionne Warwick who had a sell-out tour of the UK in 1986?
5. Who sang the words 'lick my decals off, baby' in 1970?
6. Who directed the country-music movie *Nashville*?

22

1. Prince.
2. Eddie Cochran.
3. Pete Best.
4. Roger Daltry.
5. A cappella or barber-shop singing.
6. Cliff Richard.

97

1. Winston.
2. Jerry Lee Lewis.
3. Frank Zappa.
4. Everything But the Girl.
5. Alan Freeman.
6. Donovan.

172

1. Jim Reeves.
2. The ball ('and I feel the pain', from *Runaway*).
3. Bare feet.
4. Whitney Houston.
5. Captain Beefheart.
6. Robert Altman.

23

1. Who died on 16 August 1977, aged 42?
2. Who had a UK no. 1 in 1961 with a song by Bertolt Brecht?
3. Who left Rory Storm and the Hurricanes to join the Beatles?
4. Which song by Pink Floyd contains the words 'Hey teacher! Leave us kids alone!'?
5. Which former GLC Tory councillor is also a rock historian?
6. Which band stars in the movie *Rock 'n' Roll High School*?

98

1. Who claimed 'I can sing like a frog' and was nicknamed 'Frogman'?
2. Who sang *Twenty Flight Rock* in the movie *The Girl Can't Help It*?
3. What was the Stones' first UK hit?
4. Who was lead singer of Slade?
5. Who won the 1974 Eurovision Song Contest with *Waterloo*?
6. Which pop star wrote a book entitled *After the Ball: A History of Pop*?

173

1. Which country music legend was nicknamed The Drifting Cowboy?
2. Who pleaded *I'm not a Juvenile Delinquent*?
3. Who was lead singer of the Four Tops?
4. Which sixties hero returned to the album charts in 1986 with *Back in the High Life*?
5. Which Australian band features shorts-clad guitarist Angus Young?
6. Who had a hit in 1965 with the theme from the movie *What's New, Pussycat*?

23

1. Elvis Presley.
2. Bobby Darin (the song was *Mack the Knife*).
3. Ringo.
4. *The Wall.*
5. George Tremlett.
6. The Ramones.

98

1. Clarence 'Frogman' Henry.
2. Eddie Cochran.
3. *I Wanna Be Your Man.*
4. Noddy Holder.
5. Abba.
6. Ian Whitcomb.

173

1. Hank Williams.
2. Frankie Lymon and the Teenagers.
3. Levi Stubbs.
4. Steve Winwood.
5. AC/DC.
6. Tom Jones.

24

1. Which DJ was born John Ravenscroft in Liverpool?
2. Who has been dubbed the original 'King of Shock Rock'?
3. Which supergroup made its debut before 100,000 people in Hyde Park in 1969?
4. Name the Thin Lizzy front man who died of a heroin overdose in 1986.
5. Elvis Presley is the biggest-selling recording artist of all time – next to who?
6. Which former member of the Bonzo Dog Doo Dah Band got his own TV series in 1979?

99

1. Who is Johnny Lyons better known as? (Clue: he is a big fan of the blues of Southside Chicago.)
2. Which fifties idol sported a kiss curl?
3. *Anyone Who Had a Heart*, and *You're My World* were successive UK no. 1 hits in 1964 for who?
4. Which artist includes a song in his stage repertoire entitled *Do You Think I'm Sexy*?
5. What is Mick Jagger's favourite sport?
6. Who did Wilfred Brambell portray in the Beatles movie *A Hard Day's Night*?

174

1. Who is George O'Dowd better known as?
2. Who asked *Does Your Chewing Gum Lose its Flavor on the Bedpost Overnight*?
3. Who duetted with Marvin Gaye on their 1967 hit *You're All I Need to Get By*?
4. What was the B-side of Frankie Goes To Hollywood's 1983 hit, *Relax*?
5. Who is introduced as 'The Man with the Crown'?
6. Who hosts Radio London's rock-purist show, *Echoes*?

24

1. John Peel.
2. Screaming Jay Hawkins.
3. Blind Faith.
4. Phil Lynott.
5. Bing Crosby.
6. Neil Innes (*The Innes Book of Records*).

99

1. Southside Johnny.
2. Bill Haley.
3. Cilla Black.
4. Rod Stewart.
5. Cricket.
6. Paul's grandfather.

174

1. Boy George.
2. Lonnie Donegan.
3. Tammi Terrell.
4. *Ferry Across the Mersey* (written by Gerry Marsden of Gerry and the Pacemakers).
5. James Brown.
6. Stuart Coleman.

25

1. Who was born in Duluth but raised in Hibbing, Minnesota?
2. Which rock classic was originally described as a 'novelty foxtrot'?
3. According to Scott Mackenzie, what should you wear in your hair in San Francisco?
4. Who had a hit in the UK with *Egyptian Reggae*?
5. What does CBS stand for?
6. In which movie do the kids smash up Glenn Ford's jazz records, preferring rock and roll?

100

1. Who was almost killed in a car accident while on tour in Carolina in 1973?
2. What was Elvis Presley's first job after school?
3. Who is known as 'The Night Tripper'?
4. Who had a 1974 UK hit with *W.O.L.D.* and was run over and killed in 1981?
5. What is C&W?
6. Who wrote the soundtrack to the movie *Superfly*?

175

1. Which chart-topper is a boiler-maker's daughter from Aberdeen?
2. Charles Edward Anderson Berry is also known as what?
3. Which group had five US no. 1s in a row after *Where Did Our Love Go?* in 1964?
4. Who boasted 'I live life in the bus lane'?
5. What is Helen Reddy's country of origin?
6. Who sang the title song in the movie *True Grit*?

25

1. Bob Dylan.
2. *Rock Around the Clock*.
3. Flowers.
4. Jonathan Richman.
5. Columbia Broadcasting System.
6. *Blackboard Jungle*.

100

1. Stevie Wonder.
2. Cinema usher.
3. Dr John.
4. Harry Chapin.
5. Country and Western.
6. Curtis Mayfield.

175

1. Annie Lennox.
2. Chuck Berry.
3. The Supremes.
4. Half Man Half Biscuit (*Architecture, Morality, Ted and Alice*).
5. Australia.
6. Glenn Campbell.

26

1. What group was formed in 1972 by Kevin Godley and Lol Creme?
2. Who recorded an album in 1960 entitled *The Twangs the Thang*?
3. What was the name of Peter, Paul and Mary's 'magic dragon who lived by the sea'?
4. Who first entered the charts with *Virginia Plain* in 1972?
5. What is the name for an electro-mechanical keyboard instrument designed to produce authentic sounds of strings and brass?
6. What TV show invites you to 'hold a chicken in the air'?

101

1. What rock star attempted to fly solo around the world but landed in an Indian military zone?
2. 'Giddy up, giddy up a' what?
3. Of whom did the Hollies ask 'What's your game and can anybody play'?
4. What rap crew cultivate a black-hatted outlaw image?
5. Who is the largest person ever to reach no. 1 in the charts?
6. Who starred in the TV series *The Roaring Twenties* and had a 1962 hit with *Don't Bring Lulu*?

176

1. Who was the 'Father of Soul', shot in a motel room in December 1964?
2. Which fifties crooner was married to Elizabeth Taylor?
3. What does Aretha Franklin do 'Whenever I wake up, put on my make up'?
4. Who performed pop songs based on poems by Yeats and ended up with a one-hit wonder, *Shaddup You Face*?
5. What is the only single written by John Lennon alone but not performed by him alone to go to the top?
6. What long-running TV comedy series has a theme song entitled *Suicide is Painless*?

26

1. 10 CC.
2. Duane Eddy.
3. Puff.
4. Roxy Music.
5. Mellotron.
6. Spitting Image (*The Chicken Song*).

101

1. Gary Numan.
2. 'Ding Dong'.
3. *Carrie Anne*.
4. Run DMC.
5. Demis Roussos.
6. Dorothy Provine.

176

1. Sam Cooke.
2. Eddie Fisher.
3. 'I say a little prayer for you'.
4. Joe Dolce.
5. *Jealous Guy* (Brian Ferry, 1981).
6. M.A.S.H.

27

1. Foxton, Buckler, and Weller came from Sheerwater in Surrey and formed a band called what?
2. Who was the first British performer to enter the charts straight at no. 1?
3. Who gave up being a teen idol to do washing powder commercials?
4. What was Elvis Presley's seventeenth and final UK no. 1 in 1977?
5. What Zulu folk song has been a top ten hit three times in twenty years?
6. Who combined with ELO on the theme from the film *Xanadu*?

102

1. Lead singers Ray Sawyer and Dennis Lecorriere are both known as who?
2. Who deserts Juanita to spend his time down in the cantina?
3. Where did Mick Jagger go to college?
4. Who once played a piano, organ and tone-generator for Hatfield and the North?
5. Who introduced a referee's whistle on her disco hits?
6. What movie includes *Memories are Made of This*, a hit for Dean Martin in 1956?

177

1. Who was voted Britain's most popular male vocalist in the fifties and was killed in a car crash in 1971?
2. Who wrote and performed the rock classic *Stagger Lee*?
3. Where do the Small Faces 'get high there, touch the sky there'?
4. Which best-selling singer was once Real Madrid's reserve goalkeeper?
5. Who was the first French solo singer to top the UK charts?
6. Who sang the title song for the classic western *Gunfight at the OK Corral*?

27

1. The Jam.
2. Cliff Richard.
3. Craig Douglas.
4. *Way Down.*
5. *Wimoweh (The Lion Sleeps Tonight).*
6. Olivia Newton John.

102

1. Dr Hook.
2. Speedy Gonzales.
3. London School of Economics.
4. Dave Stewart.
5. Donna Summer.
6. *The Seven Hills of Rome.*

177

1. Dicky Valentine.
2. Lloyd Price.
3. *Itchycoo Park.*
4. Julio Iglesias.
5. Charles Aznavour (with *She*).
6. Frankie Laine.

28

1. Who founded Tubeway Army?
2. 'Have gun will travel reads the card of a man'. Who?
3. Who played drums with Genesis in 1970?
4. What new wave band wore black suits, white shirts and re-introduced the Mod look?
5. What is the biggest-selling British rock album of all time?
6. What show includes the song *Stranger in Paradise*?

103

1. Who is Dino Paul Crocetti better known as?
2. Whose idea of heaven was picking a chicken?
3. Who wrote *Leaving on a Jet Plane* for Peter, Paul and Mary?
4. What duo consisting of Marc Almond and David Ball had a hit in 1981 with *Tainted Love*?
5. What are the Rock-ola 1428, the Wurlitzer 24, and the Seeburg m-100A?
6. Who entered the charts with the theme song from *Alfie*?

178

1. Who fronted The Move, ELO, and Wizzard and was born with the first name Ulysses?
2. Which fifties heart-throb was partly deaf?
3. Who gathered musicians around him in 1969 and called them his Electric Family?
4. What band urged *Don't Stand So Close to Me*?
5. Who was the first to get to the top of the UK charts with an EP?
6. What was the phrase used by John Wayne in *The Searchers* that inspired a Buddy Holly song?

28

1. Gary Numan.
2. (a man called) *Paladin.*
3. Phil Collins.
4. The Jam.
5. *Dark Side of the Moon* by Pink Floyd.
6. *Kismet.*

103

1. Dean Martin.
2. Eve Boswell (*Pickin' a Chicken*, 1956).
3. John Denver.
4. Soft Cell.
5. Juke boxes.
6. Cilla Black.

178

1. Roy Wood.
2. Johnnie Ray.
3. Jimi Hendrix.
4. Police.
5. Demis Roussos (*The Roussos Phenomenon*).
6. 'That'll be the day'.

29

1. What great jazz singer was known as 'Lady Day'?
2. Who recorded *I'm Walking Backwards for Christmas*?
3. Their most famous records were *Going Up Country* and *On the Road Again*. Who were they?
4. Tony Hadley is lead singer of which band?
5. What is the second biggest-selling UK single of all time, after *Do They Know It's Christmas*?
6. Who wrote the show *A Little Night Music*?

104

1. Who is the voice of Thomas the Tank Engine in the TV series?
2. Who in 1956 teamed up with Lionel Bart and Mike Pratt and came up with *Rock with the Cavemen*?
3. Which group had hits with *Da Doo Ron Ron*, *Then He Kissed Me*, and *He's a Rebel*?
4. Who produced and performed on a Buddy Holly tribute album entitled *Holly Days*?
5. What city is a 'lovely old queen of the sea'?
6. What musical was based on an opera by Bizet?

179

1. Who were originally called The High Numbers?
2. Who went to no. 1 in 1958 with *When*?
3. Why did the Boxtops urge 'Get me a ticket for an airplane, ain't got time for a fast train'?
4. Which disco queen once performed with the Vienna Folk Opera?
5. What was the term in the late seventies for the fusion of white punk rock and black reggae?
6. Who wrote *The Sound of Music*?

29

1. Billie Holiday.
2. The Goons.
3. Canned Heat.
4. Spandau Ballet.
5. *Mull of Kintyre* (by Wings).
6. Stephen Sondheim.

104

1. Ringo Starr.
2. Tommy Steele.
3. The Crystals.
4. Paul McCartney.
5. (Wonderful, wonderful) Copenhagen.
6. *Carmen Jones*.

179

1. The Who.
2. The Kalin twins.
3. 'cos baby wrote me a letter'.
4. Donna Summer.
5. Two Tone.
6. Rodgers and Hammerstein.

30

1. Whose signature tune is *Streets of London*?
2. Lonnie Donegan and Karl Denver both started out with which band?
3. What music spawned its own uniform of sun-bleached hair and denims cut off at the knees known as 'baggies'?
4. Who had a 1980 chart-topper with *Going Underground*?
5. Who sings about a 'dead skunk lying by the side of the road'?
6. What eight rock and roll revivalists first appeared on ITV's *New Faces*?

105

1. Who did Stephen Stills have in mind when he wrote *Suite – Judy Blue Eyes*?
2. Who gave us *We Shall Overcome* and *If I Had a Hammer*?
3. Who had nineteen chart entries between 1963 and 1969, including *Bus Stop* and *On a Carousel*?
4. What was the name of Anita Ward's suggestive hit about the visit of a telephone repair man?
5. What is the term for illicit recordings?
6. What poet wrote the sleeve notes on Bob Dylan's albums *Desire* and *Blood on the Tracks*?

180

1. What sixties group have been referred to as 'first of the heavy bands' and 'doyens of punk mysterioso'?
2. Marino Marini entered the UK charts in 1958, with *Volare*. What was his other chart success?
3. Who asked '*Do You Believe in Magic*'?
4. Who had a hit with the Tamla-Motown classic *War* in 1973?
5. In what month of what year was the Four Seasons' big night?
6. Who is Radio One's reggae DJ?

30

1. Ralph McTell.
2. Chris Barber Band.
3. Surf Music.
4. The Jam.
5. Loudon Wainwright III (*Dead Skunk*).
6. Showaddywaddy.

105

1. Judy Collins.
2. Pete Seeger.
3. The Hollies.
4. *Ring My Bell*.
5. Bootlegs.
6. Alan Ginsberg.

180

1. Vanilla Fudge.
2. *Come Prima*.
3. Lovin' Spoonful.
4. Edwin Starr.
5. *December '63*.
6. Rankin Miss P.

31

1. Who started life as Concetta Francone and became pop queen of the fifties?
2. What song written by Gilbert Becaud was a hit for Jane Morgan in 1959?
3. Who put soul to strings with *Georgia on My Mind* and *I Can't Stop Loving You*?
4. Name the Kenny Rogers saga of the Vietnam veteran no longer able to satisfy his wife.
5. What was the first single to log two million sales in the UK?
6. Who graduated from pop to star in *Catch 22* and *Carnal Knowledge*?

106

1. Who were Gaudio, Moss, DeVito and Valli?
2. Who was the first British musician to own a white Fender Stratocaster?
3. Who were the rock and roll revivalists who wore gold lamé and teddy-boy suits at the Woodstock festival?
4. Who topped the charts with a revival of Roy Orbison's *Crying* in 1980?
5. Who sings 'Heathcliff it's me, I'm Cathy come home again'?
6. Who became the first totally bald man to reach no. 1 with *If* in 1975?

181

1. Who was born Michael Barratt, in Cardiff in 1951, and played Elvis on the West End stage?
2. In The Browns' *Three Bells* whose soul wings its way to heaven?
3. What jazz giant had an unexpected no. 1 in 1968 with *Wonderful World*?
4. Who announced *I'm the Leader of the Gang*?
5. What act inspired the Clash song *Guns on the Roof (of the World)*?
6. What country star featured in *Oh God* with George Burns?

31

1. Connie Francis.
2. *The Day That the Rains Came.*
3. Ray Charles.
4. *Ruby Don't Take Your Love to Town.*
5. *Mull of Kintyre* (by Wings).
6. Art Garfunkel.

106

1. The Four Seasons.
2. Hank Marvin.
3. Sha na na.
4. Don McLean.
5. Kate Bush (in *Wuthering Heights*).
6. Telly Savalas.

181

1. Shakin' Stevens.
2. Jimmy Brown.
3. Louis Armstrong.
4. Gary Glitter.
5. Two members of the band were taken to court for shooting racing pigeons on a roof in Camden Town.
6. John Denver.

32

1. Vince Furnier was the first transexual shock-rocker. Who is she better known as?
2. Name the Everly Brothers clones who topped the charts in 1961 with *Are You Sure*?
3. Who had a hit with *Bend Me, Shape Me* in 1968?
4. Who is the real Roxanne?
5. What is the term for a rough cutting of a record on a metal plate for demo purposes?
6. Who was dismissed as a Radio One DJ in 1970 following remarks about a transport minister's wife?

107

1. Who has been described as 'The deranged first lady of Kooky-pop'?
2. What comedian first entered the hit parade with *Love is Like a Violin*?
3. Where was it that a man was stabbed to death by Hell's Angels before 400,000 Rolling Stones fans in 1969?
4. What metropolitan authority organized an Easter Reggae Festival on the South Bank in 1985?
5. What is the term for the sound produced by a guitar or microphone picking up its own emanations when in close proximity to a speaker.
6. Who composed the original James Bond theme?

182

1. Who is Michael Jackson's hit-making sister?
2. In Eddie Cochran's *Three Steps to Heaven*, what is Step Two?
3. Who entered the charts for the first and only time with *She's not There*?
4. What does CD stand for?
5. What theatre in Harlem, New York, has for decades been a showcase for black entertainers?
6. Which orchestral arranger and conductor got into the charts in 1960 with the theme from *A Summer Place*?

32

1. Alice Cooper.
2. The Allisons.
3. Amen Corner.
4. This is a subject of endless debate in the world of hip-pop. Answer: The Real Roxanne or Roxanne Shante.
5. Acetate.
6. Kenny Everett.

107

1. Cyndi Lauper.
2. Ken Dodd.
3. Altamont.
4. The GLC.
5. (Negative) feedback.
6. John Barry.

182

1. Janet.
2. 'She falls in love with you'.
3. Zombies.
4. Compact Discs.
5. Apollo.
6. Percy Faith.

33

1. By what name is Terence Nelhans better known?
2. Where does Lonnie Donegan's old man, the dustman, live?
3. Which band invented the phrase 'life in the fast lane'?
4. Which eighties superstar once hosted a Saturday morning cartoon show?
5. Who nursed her lead guitarist for five years while he lay stricken with pemphigus?
6. Who played teen idol Cookie in TV's *77 Sunset Strip*?

108

1. Who is still known as 'Rod the Mod'?
2. How old was Buddy Holly when he died?
3. Who was hailed as a 13-year-old genius and as the new Ray Charles?
4. Who was lead singer with the Boomtown Rats in 1980?
5. What is the name for country blues music sung in Louisiana patois?
6. Who composed the title tune for the Bond movie *Goldfinger*?

183

1. By what name were Bobby Hatfield and Bill Medley better known?
2. Who fronted the MGs?
3. Name the original Supreme who ended up on welfare and died in 1976.
4. Who urged us all to stay in the YMCA?
5. Which tune did Randy Newman originally write for Frank Sinatra?
6. Which movie featured music by Ry Cooder and Buffy Saint Marie and starred Mick Jagger?

33

1. Adam Faith.
2. In a council flat (from Donegan's hit *My Old Man's a Dustman*).
3. The Eagles.
4. Michael Jackson (then with the Jackson Five).
5. Debbie Harry (the guitarist was Chris Stein of Blondie).
6. Ed Byrne.

108

1. Rod Stewart.
2. 22.
3. Stevie Wonder.
4. Bob Geldof.
5. Cajun.
6. Paul McCartney.

183

1. The Righteous Brothers.
2. Booker T.
3. Florence Ballard.
4. Village People.
5. *Lonely at the Top.*
6. *Performance.*

34

1. Who was known as 'Big O'?
2. Who wore black leather and an eyepatch and was killed in a car crash?
3. Who went to the top in 1965 with *Concrete and Clay*?
4. Who replaced Mick Taylor during the Rolling Stones' US tour of 1975?
5. Who coined the term 'plastic soul'?
6. Who originally recorded *Don't Cry for me, Argentina* from *Evita*, before the show was premiered in the West End?

109

1. Who was known as 'The Poet Laureate of Rock'?
2. *Chapel of the Roses*, *St Theresa of the Roses*, and *My Special Angel* were all the work of who?
3. Which pseudo-psychedelic band became a cult after the release of a tape of an 'untogether' recording session?
4. Rat Scabies is a founder member of what band?
5. Who introduces his show as the JY Prog?
6. Who sings the title song of *Minder*?

184

1. Who styles herself 'The Divine Miss M'?
2. Johnny Tillotson had a UK no. 1 in 1960 with *Poetry in Motion*. What were his other chart-busters?
3. What band, formed in 1966, made their name touring with Andy Warhol's Plastic Exploding Inevitable?
4. Which band features guitarist Johnny Marr?
5. What was Motown's first gold record?
6. Who wrote *Come and Get It* for the movie *The Magic Christian*?

34

1. Roy Orbison.
2. Johnny Kidd.
3. Unit 4+2.
4. Ron Wood.
5. David Bowie.
6. Julie Covington.

109

1. Chuck Berry.
2. Malcolm Vaughan.
3. The Troggs.
4. The Damned.
5. Jimmy Young.
6. Dennis Waterman.

184

1. Bette Midler.
2. He didn't have any.
3. Velvet Underground.
4. The Smiths.
5. *Shop Around*, by Smokey Robinson and The Miracles.
6. Paul McCartney.

35

1. Who was born Steve Georgiou and later converted to Islam?
2. What instrument did Eddie Calvert play?
3. Who went to no. 1 in the UK charts in 1969 with *Where do You Go to, My Lovely*?
4. Which member of the Conservative Party Youth Committee manages the Police?
5. Who was found dead in his swimming pool in his luxury home in Sussex?
6. A film actress and her husband went to no. 1 in 1969 with *Je t'aime moi non plus*. Who were they?

110

1. Robert Bell fronts what band?
2. 'Volare, oh! oh!' What is the next line?
3. Who founded Led Zeppelin?
4. Who said 'The Smiths are great by definition. Everything we produce is wonderful'?
5. When you move right up close to me, what happens?
6. Who wrote the theme music for *Superman* and *Star Wars*?

185

1. Who is Clementina Campbell better known as?
2. Who was Neil Sedaka's 1959 *Oh! Carol* dedicated to?
3. What pioneer of the Mersey Beat had his last hit in 1965 with *Trains and Boats and Planes*?
4. Which member of The Stranglers went to prison for drug possession?
5. Who retired from music to run a Nazi war memorabilia shop in North London?
6. Which teen idol starred in *The Alamo* with John Wayne?

35

1. Cat Stevens.
2. Trumpet.
3. Peter Sarstedt.
4. Miles Copeland.
5. Brian Jones.
6. Jane Birkin and Serge Gainsbourg.

110

1. Kool and the Gang.
2. 'Cantare oh! oh!'.
3. Jimmy Page.
4. Morrissey.
5. 'That's when I get the shakes all over me' (*Shakin' All Over*).
6. John Williams.

185

1. Cleo Laine.
2. Carole King.
3. Billy J. Kramer.
4. Hugh Cornwell.
5. Chris Farlowe.
6. Frankie Avalon.

36

1. Who was the first 'Singing Cowboy'?
2. What was Cliff Richard's first hit?
3. Which sixties guitar hero once played with Little Richard?
4. Which British soul band is fronted by Errol Brown?
5. What is inscribed on Phil Spector's father's gravestone?
6. Who appeared as a housewife in the 1979 movie *Union City*?

111

1. Who is Kim Wilde's dad?
2. Who was arrested outside Elvis's mansion brandishing a pistol?
3. Which group was founded by Alan Clarke and Graham Nash?
4. What was The Specials' home town?
5. What is the link between the 1967 chart success *There Must Be a Way* and Frankie Goes to Hollywood?
6. Who sings the title tune in the movie *Mona Lisa*?

186

1. Who is acclaimed as 'King of Redneck Rock'?
2. Where is Buddy Holly's home town?
3. Who did the Beatles visit in India in 1967?
4. Who had his only chart success with a cover version of George Harrison's *Here Comes The Sun* in 1971?
5. With what sound is Chet Atkins associated?
6. Who played the leader of the Mods in the movie *Quadrophenia*?

36

1. Gene Autry.
2. *Move It*.
3. Jimi Hendrix.
4. Hot Chocolate.
5. To Know Him is to Love Him (after his hit with The Teddybears).
6. Debbie Harry.

111

1. Marty Wilde.
2. Jerry Lee Lewis.
3. The Hollies.
4. Coventry.
5. The song was by Frankie Vaughan, whose visit to Hollywood inspired the group's name.
6. Nat King Cole.

186

1. Willie Nelson.
2. Lubbock, Texas.
3. The Maharishi.
4. Richie Havens.
5. The Nashville sound.
6. Sting.

37

1. Whose middle name was Nesta?
2. Which legendary song-writing team wrote *Riot in Cell Block No. 9* and *Smoky Joe's Cafe*?
3. Which Beatles album concludes with an endless final chord?
4. Which eighties New York cult band features miniskirts, go-go boots, toy instruments, the *Camel Walk* and *The Sly Tuna*?
5. What is the word for heavily amplified, over the top, electric-guitar-dominated rock?
6. Who starred in *Don't Knock the Rock*?

112

1. Who was J. P. Richardson better known as?
2. Who covered the US hit *Willy and the Hand Jive* in Britain?
3. Which instrument was played by Dave Clark of the Dave Clark 5?
4. Which performance artist had a hit with her 1981 rendering of *O Superman*?
5. Which country singer wears a red bandana?
6. What was the theme song from the movie *Butch Cassidy and the Sundance Kid*?

187

1. Which early sixties teen idol was promoted as 'Tiger Man'?
2. Who got a job with the Crown Electric Company as a truck driver in 1953?
3. Which mod band led by Andy Fairweather Lowe had a hit with *(If Paradise is) Half as Nice*?
4. Who had a disco hit with a cut up of a Vietnam war documentary?
5. Why was Greg Allman shunned by his band in 1976?
6. Who hosted Radio London's rock purist show *Honky Tonk*?

37

1. Bob Marley.
2. Jerry Lieber and Mike Stoller.
3. *Sgt Pepper* (the track is *A Day in the Life*).
4. The B-52s.
5. Heavy Metal.
6. Bill Haley.

112

1. The Big Bopper.
2. Cliff Richard.
3. Drums.
4. Laurie Anderson.
5. Willie Nelson.
6. *Raindrops Keep Falling on My Head.*

187

1. Fabian.
2. Elvis.
3. Amen Corner.
4. Paul Hardcastle.
5. Because he helped get his roadie sent to prison for seventy-five years for drug dealing.
6. Charlie Gillett.

38

1. What is DJ Alan Freeman's nickname?
2. Who proposed to Maria Elena Santiago on their very first date?
3. Who announced 'When I say I'm in luv, I'm in luv L–U–V'?
4. Whose first chart success was *Run Rabbit* in 1980?
5. Is Norrie Paramour a) a pacific island b) patois for new love c) a record producer?
6. Who went to Hollywood from Canada at 14 and composed the music for *The Longest Day*?

113

1. Whose signature tune is *Fever*?
2. Who was shot and wounded by a female friend in a New York Hotel in 1961, and had a heart attack on stage in 1975?
3. What band had Friday on their minds?
4. Who scored with a remake of the Everly Brothers' classic *When Will I be Loved*?
5. In which country will you find only one recording label, Melodiya Records?
6. Who co-starred with Peter Sellers in the film *The Magic Christian*?

188

1. Who was awarded the MBE in 1965 and returned it in 1969?
2. Who advertised his foolproof system for winning the pools on Radio Luxemburg?
3. A butcher's son formed the Tremeloes then went back to the shop. Who was he?
4. Which rock entertainer is always making a *Beautiful Noise*?
5. Who originated Afro-beat and married twenty-seven female singers and dancers giving him twenty-eight wives?
6. Which novelist originally coined the phrase 'heavy metal'?

38

1. Fluff.
2. Buddy Holly.
3. Shangri-Las.
4. Chas and Dave.
5. c) Record producer.
6. Paul Anka.

113

1. Peggy Lee.
2. Jackie Wilson.
3. Wayne Fontana and the Mindbenders.
4. Linda Ronstadt.
5. USSR.
6. Ringo Starr.

188

1. John Lennon.
2. Horace Bachelor.
3. Brian Poole.
4. Neil Diamond.
5. Fela Kuti.
6. William Burroughs (in *The Naked Lunch*).

39

1. Which ex shock rocker heads a political party?
2. What was the name of Liberace's brother?
3. Who was only 14 when her record *Shout* went to no. 1?
4. Who wrote *Season of the Witch*?
5. Who is Prince Charles's favourite group?
6. Who wrote and recorded the title song for the movie *Absolute Beginners*?

114

1. Which Rolling Stone is the son of a lorry driver?
2. What was Tommy Steele's first hit?
3. What is Gram Parsons acknowledged to be the creator of?
4. Who topped the charts in 1985 with *Frankie*?
5. What were Nancy Sinatra's boots made for?
6. Who wrote a book about the Beatles called *Shout!*?

189

1. Who is Paul Raven better known as?
2. Who died when his aircraft exploded due to people trying to freebase on board?
3. Her greatest record, *My Guy*, came out in 1964. Who was she?
4. Who had polio at seven, went to the Royal College of Art and formed a band called Kilburn and the High Roads?
5. Who had a major hit with 'if you got a problem . . . *I Can Help*'?
6. Which musical includes *Some Enchanted Evening*?

39

1. Screaming Lord Sutch (Raving Loony Monster Party).
2. George.
3. Lulu.
4. Donovan.
5. The Three Degrees.
6. David Bowie.

114

1. Charlie Watts.
2. *Singing the Blues*.
3. Country Rock.
4. Sister Sledge.
5. Walking.
6. Philip Norman.

189

1. Gary Glitter.
2. Ricky Nelson.
3. Mary Wells.
4. Ian Dury.
5. Billy Swan.
6. *South Pacific*.

40

1. Who was born Charles Westover in 1939 and wrote *Hats Off to Larry* and *Keep Searchin*?
2. Who first made the charts in 1959 with *What Do You Want to Make Those Eyes at Me for*?
3. Who were discovered by Chris Lambert playing in a Shepherd's Bush pub in 1964?
4. Who are PIL?
5. What do scientists predict will render vinyl records obsolete well before the year 2000?
6. What band is featured in the film *Flame* (1975)?

115

1. Which distinguished blues/rock guitarist is an albino?
2. How many top twenty entries did Lonnie Donegan have between 1956 and 1962?
3. Who was 'Tall and tanned and young and lovely'?
4. Which Grandmaster fronts the Furious Five?
5. Which city gave birth to jazz?
6. Who composed the soundtrack for *McKenna's Gold*?

190

1. Who were 'Kenny 'n' Cash' on Pirate Radio London?
2. Who was star vocalist with The Ted Heath Band?
3. Who was the Beatles' manager?
4. Which 'super sideman' of the early seventies wore a top hat over long wispy hair and beard?
5. 'What do you want if you don't want money?' Next line?
6. Which pop entrepreneur had a whole South Bank Show devoted to him?

40

1. Del Shannon.
2. Emile Ford and the Checkmates.
3. The Who.
4. Public Image Limited.
5. Compact Discs.
6. Slade.

115

1. Johnny Winter.
2. 26.
3. *The Girl from Ipanema.*
4. Grandmaster Flash with Melle Mel.
5. New Orleans.
6. Jose Feliciano.

190

1. Kenny Everett and Dave Cash.
2. Denis Lotis.
3. Brian Epstein.
4. Leon Russell.
5. 'What do you want if you don't want dough?' (*What do You Want?*).
6. Malcolm McLaren.

41

1. Which pop star's family is descended from the Huguenots?
2. Who wanted a robot man to hold her tight?
3. Which US DJ was known as 'The Fifth Beatle'?
4. Who sing about 'heavy metal thunder' in *Born to be Wild*?
5. What was the Princess of Wales rumoured to have hummed on the way to her wedding?
6. Which Willie Russell show starring Barbara Dickson was voted Musical of the Year in 1983?

116

1. Who 'killed him a bear' when he was only three?
2. Who was a *Big Man* yesterday?
3. What psychedelic ditty features a child describing flying on the back of an albatross?
4. Peter Cetera left which band to go solo in 1985?
5. What kinky article of clothing did Honor Blackman sing about?
6. Can you name Paul McCartney's expensive 1985 movie flop?

191

1. Whose path was beaten bare with footsteps leading to his cabin?
2. If you miss the last train to San Fernando, what's the problem?
3. Wink Martindale is best known in Britain for which song?
4. According to RCA President Robert Sumner, what threatens the viability of the music business as we know it?
5. What is Barry Manilow's most prominent feature?
6. What was the rock musical version of Joseph and his coat of many colours?

41

1. Simon Le Bon.
2. Connie Francis.
3. Murray the K.
4. Steppenwolf.
5. *Just One Cornetto.*
6. *Bloodbrothers.*

116

1. Davy Crockett.
2. The Four Preps.
3. *Letting in Water* (Traffic).
4. Chicago.
5. *Kinky Boots.*
6. *Give My Regards to Broad Street.*

191

1. (The son of) Hickory Hollis (Tramp).
2. You'll never get another one.
3. *Deck of Cards.*
4. Home taping.
5. His nose.
6. *Joseph and His Amazing Technicolor Dreamcoat.*

42

1. Who did Robert Zimmerman turn into?
2. Which British comic had a hit with a cover version of Bobby Darin's *Splish Splash*?
3. Who do the Beatles say was 'so good looking she looked like a man'?
4. Who left the Modern Lovers to join the Talking Heads?
5. What punk band was led by Joe Strummer?
6. Who played Buddy Holly in the movie *The Buddy Holly Story*?

117

1. Slim Jim Phantom, Lee Rocker and Brian Setzer were once known as what?
2. Where was Elvis Presley born?
3. What was DJ John Peel's show on pirate Radio London?
4. Which ex Bronski Beat is lead singer of the Communards?
5. *The Girl from Ipanema* and *Desafinado* were examples of which sound?
6. Who starred in the rock movie *Stardust*?

192

1. Henry John Deutschendorfer is better known as who?
2. Who wrote *Blue Suede Shoes*?
3. Which rock star constantly referred to both his living parents as having died?
4. In the band Echo and the Bunnymen, who or what is 'Echo'?
5. What nationality is Nana Moskouri?
6. Who played together for the last time in the movie *The Last Waltz*?

42

1. Bob Dylan.
2. Charlie Drake.
3. *Polythene Pam.*
4. Jerry Harrison.
5. The Clash.
6. Gary Busey.

117

1. Stray Cats.
2. Tupelo, Mississippi.
3. The Perfumed Garden.
4. Jimmy Somerville.
5. Bossa nova.
6. David Essex.

192

1. John Denver.
2. Carl Perkins.
3. Jim Morrison.
4. The drum-machine (now dispensed with).
5. Greek.
6. The Band.

43

1. Which DJ is known as The Emperor?
2. Who was Elvis Presley's manager?
3. Who made the three best-selling singles in the UK in 1967?
4. Who had their first chart success in 1977 with *So You Win Again*?
5. Who is Queen's lead singer?
6. Who composed the music for *The Colour Purple*?

118

1. Who records with daughters Laury, Trudy, Cherry, and Debby, and wife Shirley?
2. Which two Chuck Berry classics were covered by the Beatles?
3. What was the B side of *Strawberry Fields Forever*?
4. Nile Rodgers and Bernie Edwards were the brains behind which disco creation?
5. The Royal Scots Dragoon Guards had a UK no. 1 in 1972 with which tune?
6. Who composed the music for *Little Fauss and Big Halsey*?

193

1. They hailed from Leighton Buzzard, Baron Anthony on bass. Who were they?
2. Who told Eddie Cochran in *Summertime Blues* 'I'd love to help you son by you're too young to vote'?
3. Who left the Hollies to join Crosby, Stills and Young?
4. How did Hall and Oates first meet?
5. What is James Taylor's signature tune?
6. Who composed and sang the music for the movie *O Lucky Man*?

43

1. Emperor Rosco.
2. Colonel Parker.
3. Engelbert Humperdinck.
4. Hot Chocolate.
5. Freddie Mercury.
6. Quincy Jones.

118

1. Pat Boone.
2. *Roll Over Beethoven* and *Rock and Roll Music*.
3. *Penny Lane*.
4. Chic.
5. *Amazing Grace*.
6. Johnny Cash and Carl Perkins.

193

1. The Barron Knights.
2. His Congressman.
3. Graham Nash.
4. They met in a lift while escaping a gang-fight at the Adelphi Ballroom, Philadelphia.
5. *Fire and Rain*.
6. Alan Price.

44

1. Trevor Stanford DSM, who lost a finger-top in the navy, played piano under what name?
2. Who had hits in the fifties with *Let Me Go, Lover*, and *Sweet Old-Fashioned Girl*?
3. What Beatles ditty starts 'I once met a girl, or should I say she once met me'?
4. What is the name for adoring young girls who attach themselves to their pop heroes?
5. What group prompted one critic to write 'If they make it I'll have to commit suicide'?
6. Who directed and stars in *True Stories* (1986)?

119

1. Who does the *Crocodile Rock*?
2. How much is that doggy in the window?
3. Who was the leader of the Lovin' Spoonful who pleaded *Darlin' Be Home Soon*?
4. What is the term for playing guitar with a piece of metal or glass slid up and down the fretboard?
5. Who was the first person to sing in German on a no. 1 hit?
6. In what musical does Mitzi Gaynor 'wash that man right out of her hair'?

194

1. Who are Teddy, Joy and Babs better known as?
2. Who or what was a Dansette?
3. Who went to no. 1 in 1968 with *Mony Mony*?
4. Who had a hit in 1979 with *When You're in Love with a Beautiful Woman*?
5. Which Beatles song spells LSD?
6. Who played a mad drummer in the film *Stardust*?

44

1. Russ Conway.
2. Teresa Brewer.
3. *Norwegian Wood.*
4. Groupies.
5. Uriah Heep.
6. David Byrne.

119

1. Elton John.
2. Nobody knows.
3. John Sebastian.
4. Bottlenecking.
5. Elvis Presley (*Wooden Heart*).
6. *South Pacific.*

194

1. The Beverley Sisters.
2. A record player.
3. Tommy James and the Shondells.
4. Dr Hook.
5. *Lucy in the Sky with Diamonds.*
6. Keith Moon.

45

1. In which group did Nina Von Pallandt appear?
2. In which song can the Everly Brothers 'taste your lips of wine, anytime, night or day'?
3. Who had a hit with *Sidesaddle*?
4. Which duo like rock and roll, pie and mash, and stewed eels?
5. 'Went to the dance looking for romance'. Who did I see?
6. Who wrote the musical *Fings Ain't What They Used to Be*?

120

1. Where was Davy Crockett born?
2. Which Peter Sellers/Spike Milligan duet begins 'When I was a little baby'?
3. Who entered the UK charts with *Tous les garçons*?
4. Who sings about werewolves of London and headless gunners?
5. Feargal Sharkey was the lead singer of which band?
6. Who regularly plays Peter Pan since her first hit *Loving You* in 1967?

195

1. Where did Donovan's *Jennifer Juniper* live?
2. Which soccer star was a contestant on *Double Your Money* answering questions on pop?
3. Who had a hit in 1968 with a cover of the Beatles' *Lady Madonna*?
4. Name the Mormon family who became teenybop idols in the seventies?
5. Seven little girls 'sitting in the back seat kissing and a-hugging' with whom?
6. Who admitted in a David Frost TV interview that he preferred soccer to pop?

45

1. Nina and Frederick.
2. *All You Have to Do is Dream.*
3. Russ Conway.
4. Chas and Dave.
5. *Barbara Ann.*
6. Lionel Bart.

120

1. 'On a mountain top in Tennessee'.
2. *The Ying Tong Song.*
3. Françoise Hardy.
4. Warren Zevon.
5. The Undertones.
6. Anita Harris.

195

1. Up on the hill.
2. Bobby Charlton.
3. Fats Domino.
4. The Osmonds.
5. Fred.
6. Elton John.

46

1. Who is Gordon Sumner now known as?
2. Which fifties classic has the refrain 'Life could be a dream'?
3. Who in 1967 were described as Australian rock's answer to the Beatles and Stones?
4. Who played a mixture of ska, rock and Motown which they called 'The Nutty Sound'?
5. What is the term for spoken and semi-sung verse over powerful rhythm tracks?
6. Who played Billy Liar in the musical *Billy*?

121

1. Who wrote his own epitaph for his gravestone: 'Please don't judge me too harshly'?
2. When this old world starts getting me down, and people are just too much for me to take, where do I go?
3. Who had a UK no. 1 with *Do-Wah-Diddy*?
4. Which David Bowie song ends 'Wham bam thank you Ma'am'?
5. Who had their own record label, Rockney?
6. Who played the poet Byron at the Young Vic in 1981?

196

1. What is Tommy Steele's real name?
2. Which Neil Sedaka hit took his girl through the year citing a new attribute for each month?
3. What sacred religious chant entered the charts in 1969?
4. Who staged a free concert in Hyde Park for Jubilee Year and attracted 150,000 fans?
5. Who recorded a song entitled *My Head Hurts, My Feet Stink and I Don't Believe in Jesus*?
6. Who attempted a comeback with the theme from the film *Champions* in 1984?

46

1. Sting.
2. *Sha-boom.*
3. The Easybeats.
4. Madness.
5. Rap.
6. Michael Crawford.

121

1. Brian Jones.
2. *Up on the Roof.*
3. Manfred Mann.
4. *Suffragette City.*
5. Chas and Dave.
6. David Essex.

196

1. Thomas Hicks.
2. *Calendar Girl.*
3. *Hare Krishna.*
4. Queen.
5. Jimmy Buffin.
6. Shirley Bassey.

47

1. Who was the youngest member of the Osmond family?
2. Who was king of the discotheques in 1962 with *Let's Dance*?
3. Who topped the charts in 1966 with *You Don't Have to Say You Love Me*?
4. Who in the late seventies were 'Gay goofs to those who got the joke and disco novelties to those who didn't'?
5. What did Keith Richard say was the most exciting moment of his life?
6. Which classical composer made it to the pop charts with the theme from *2001 – A Space Odyssey*?

122

1. Who were Jones, Bonham, Page and Plant better known as?
2. Long-distance information, gimme where?
3. Who invited us to a Beggars' Banquet?
4. Who recorded *White Punks on Dope* featuring Quay Lewd?
5. Who, according to Randy Newman, had an amazing dancing bear?
6. Who wrote a warts-and-all biography of Elvis Presley entitled *Elvis*?

197

1. Who in the fifties was Britain's 'King of the Electric Guitar'?
2. What does Pat Boone spend time writing in the sand?
3. 'There she goes with her nose in the air'. What is the next line?
4. Who was lead singer of The Jam?
5. Who formed their own record company, Rocket Records?
6. Who wrote a play about rock power fantasies called *Tooth of Crime*?

47

1. Little Jimmy.
2. Chris Montez.
3. Dusty Springfield.
4. Village People.
5. Appearing on the same stage as Little Richard.
6. Johann Strauss.

122

1. Led Zeppelin.
2. *Memphis, Tennessee*.
3. The Rolling Stones.
4. Tubes.
5. Simon Smith.
6. Albert Goldman.

197

1. Bert Weedon.
2. Love letters.
3. 'Funny how love can be' (*Ivy League*).
4. Paul Weller.
5. Elton John and Bernie Taupin.
6. Sam Shephard.

48

1. What is the family name of sisters June, Ruth, and Anita?
2. Who entered the UK charts only once with the immortal *At the Hop*?
3. Who demanded: 'Scuse me while I kiss the sky'?
4. What country does heavy metal band Loudness come from?
5. What religion has been the main inspiration behind the development of reggae music?
6. Who got an Oscar in 1971 for the theme from *Shaft*?

123

1. What crooner is always leaving his heart in San Francisco?
2. Whose version of *Why* went to the top in the UK in 1959?
3. According to the Ronettes, what is the best part of breaking up?
4. Who updated *Space Oddity* with *Ashes, the Continuing Story of Major Tom*?
5. According to songwriters Keller and Sedaka, what colour are Venus's jeans?
6. What musical is based on poems by T. S. Eliot?

198

1. Who was the fifties 'Queen of the Ivories' with *Poor People of Paris*?
2. Who recorded a song entitled *Never Do a Tango With an Eskimo*?
3. What was James Darren's one and only UK hit, in 1962?
4. Who at 51 became the oldest woman to make a chart debut with *My Toot Toot*?
5. Who sang 'God save little shops, china cups and virginity'?
6. Who wrote a musical about Sweeny Todd?

48

1. Pointer Sisters.
2. Danny and the Juniors.
3. Jimi Hendrix.
4. Japan.
5. Rastafarianism.
6. Isaac Hayes.

123

1. Tony Bennett.
2. Anthony Newley.
3. Making up.
4. David Bowie.
5. Blue (*Venus in Blue Jeans*).
6. *Cats*.

198

1. Winifred Atwell.
2. Alma Cogan.
3. *Goodbye Cruel World*.
4. Denise LaSalle (in 1985).
5. The Kinks.
6. Stephen Sondheim.

49

1. Who was Cass Eliot better known as?
2. Whose UK cover version of *Wake Up Little Suzy* rivalled the Everly Brothers'?
3. Who deputized for Ringo on a Beatles world tour?
4. What sound is associated with the Def Jam label?
5. What did Cliff Richard put in a trunk so no big hunk could steal?
6. Who had an album hit with songs from *Mary Poppins*?

124

1. Whose signature tune was *Mountain Greenery*?
2. Why was Easter Sunday 1960 a black day for rock and roll?
3. Who wrote a 1965 hit with husband Tony Hatch, *Where Are You Now, My Love*?
4. Which Swindon-based band were once known as the Helium Kidz and feature Andy Partridge?
5. Who made an album entitled *Sir Henry of Rawlinson End*?
6. Which respected singer/songwriter used to appear in the TV series M.A.S.H.?

199

1. Who went *Way Down Yonder in New Orleans* and was nicknamed 'Boom Boom'?
2. Whose peculiar vocal style ensured a hit for *Good Timing*?
3. Which Aussie favourite had a 1969 tearjerker success with *Two Little Boys*?
4. Who stayed at no. 1 for seven weeks in 1970 with *In the Summertime*?
5. Which ex Rolling Stone financed and organized his own full-size jazz swing orchestra?
6. Which Scottish balladeer had his own BBC show and always wore a kilt?

49

1. Mama Cass.
2. The King Brothers.
3. Jimmy Nicol.
4. Hip-hop.
5. A *Living Doll*.
6. Julie Andrews.

124

1. Mel Torme.
2. Eddie Cochran was killed in a car crash on that day.
3. Jackie Trent.
4. XTC.
5. Viv Stanshall.
6. Loudon Wainwright III.

199

1. Freddie Cannon.
2. Jimmy Jones.
3. Rolf Harris.
4. Mungo Jerry.
5. Charlie Watts.
6. Andy Stewart.

50

1. Name the 'Father of British Blues' who died in 1985.
2. Who in the fifties had a following second only to Elvis?
3. Why was Jim Morrison sentenced to six months hard labour in 1969?
4. Who went to no. 1 in 1985 with *When the Going Gets Tough*?
5. Which soccer manager gets a mention on the Beatles album *Let It Be*?
6. Who composed the score for the film *Green Ice* in 1980?

125

1. Who is Martha Reeves better known as?
2. Who was Polish America's answer to Elvis Presley?
3. Which former member of the Byrds is now a born-again Christian?
4. Who skippered a boat called *Drum* in the 1985 Fastnet race?
5. What does HMV stand for?
6. Who produced the TV rock music series *Boy Meets Girl*?

200

1. Who sings 'I wear black for the poor and beaten down', and is known as 'The Man in Black'?
2. Which fifties hit starts 'In 1814 we took a little trip'?
3. Who had a UK no. 1 with *My Boy Lollipop*?
4. Who sings about Interpol and DeutscheBank, FBI and Scotland Yard?
5. If you mix rock and country what do you get?
6. Who wrote the soundtrack for the movie *Pat Garrett and Billy the Kid*?

50

1. Alexis Korner.
2. Pat Boone.
3. For flashing on stage in Miami (an act which gained him the nickname 'The Miami Flash').
4. Billy Ocean.
5. Sir Matt Busby.
6. Bill Wyman.

125

1. Martha and the Vandellas.
2. Bobby Vinton.
3. Roger McGuinn.
4. Simon Le Bon.
5. His Master's Voice.
6. Jack Good.

200

1. Johnny Cash.
2. *The Battle of New Orleans*.
3. Millie.
4. Kraftwerk (on their album *Computerworld*).
5. Rockabilly.
6. Bob Dylan.

51

1. Who married George Jones in 1968 and wrote a hit about their divorce in 1975?
2. What was the flip side of Elvis's 1959 no. 1 *Hound Dog*?
3. Who described himself as the only guitarist to have left the Stones and lived?
4. Which 80s chart-topper is half Nigerian?
5. Which female singer's grandfather was a Nobel Prize winner?
6. Who hosted *Juke Box Jury*?

126

1. Mike McGear of Scaffold started life as who?
2. Which operatic tenor had a popular hit with *O Sole Mio*?
3. Name the Wichita Linesman who once stood in for Brian Wilson of the Beach Boys.
4. What is London's biggest gay disco?
5. Who produced *It's My Party* by Leslie Gore?
6. Who made an inspired parody of a Beatles film called *All You Need is Cash*?

201

1. Karen Woodward, Siobhan Fahey and Sarah Dallin are better known as what?
2. 'You load 16 tons and what do you get?'
3. Who played drums in Emerson, Lake and Palmer?
4. In what year did Phil Collins release his first solo album?
5. With what kind of music do you associate Murray Cash?
6. Who directed *American Graffiti*?

51

1. Tammy Wynnette.
2. *Don't Be Cruel.*
3. Mick Taylor.
4. Sade.
5. Olivia Newton John.
6. David Jacobs.

126

1. Mike McCartney (brother of Paul).
2. Mario Lanza.
3. Glen Campbell.
4. Heaven.
5. Quincy Jones.
6. Eric Idle.

201

1. Bananarama.
2. 'Another day older and deeper in debt' (*16 Tons*).
3. Carl Palmer.
4. 1981.
5. Country and Western.
6. George Lucas.

52

1. Who started life as Frederick Bulsara, was born in Zanzibar in 1949, and is a qualified graphic designer?
2. Which Radio 2 DJ was once in the top ten with *Chain Gang*?
3. Name the Pink Floyd song about a boy who stole women's underwear.
4. How many were there in Madness?
5. Who went to no. 1 with *The Ballad of Bonnie and Clyde*?
6. Hugo Montenegro topped the charts in 1968 with the theme music from which spaghetti western?

127

1. Charles Hughes and Dave Peacock are also known as who?
2. Which TV comedian made a cover version of Dean Martin's *Memories are Made of This* in 1956?
3. Who took us for a *Walk In the Black Forest*?
4. Who was responsible for *C30 C60 C90 Go!* and *Sexy Eiffel Tower*?
5. What Irish group has been described as 'a singing sisterhood of set smiles and musical syrup'?
6. Who got her first break in 1973 when asked by Willie Russell to play in *John, Paul, George, Ringo and Bert*?

202

1. Who is the singing guitarist with the Blow Monkeys?
2. Which singer/comic's byline is 'I wanna tell you a story'?
3. Who shouts 'All right, George!' just before the guitar break on the Beatles' *Boys*?
4. Who had a 1978 hit album entitled *Parallel Lines*?
5. Who leads the Northern Variety Orchestra?
6. Alan Price and Tom Courtenay collaborated in a stage musical about which cartoon character?

52

1. Freddie Mercury.
2. Jimmy Young.
3. *Arnold Layne*.
4. Seven.
5. Georgie Fame.
6. *The Good, the Bad and the Ugly*.

127

1. Chas and Dave.
2. Dave King.
3. Horst Jankowski.
4. Malcolm McLaren.
5. The Nolans.
6. Barbara Dickson.

202

1. Dr Robert.
2. Max Bygraves.
3. Ringo.
4. Blondie.
5. Alyn Ainsworth.
6. Andy Capp.

53

1. Who was born Mark Feld, son of a taxi driver, in 1948?
2. Name the Irish heart-throb who made it big with *Roses Are Red.*
3. Who are the only American psychedelic rock band to survive into the eighties?
4. What did rock-steady turn into in the late sixties?
5. Who is described by Tommy Roe as having blue eyes and a pony tail, and cheeks like posies?
6. Which TV rock show was originally presented by Paula Yates and Jools Holland?

128

1. Who proclaimed himself 'Soul Brother Number One'?
2. Which bandleader's catchphrase was 'Wakey, Wakey'?
3. Whose first chart success in 1967 was entitled *New York Mining Disaster 1941*?
4. Who was the top-selling female vocalist in the UK in 1975?
5. Who is responsible for records credited to bands with such tasteful names as Scraping Foetus off the Wheel, You've Got Foetus on Your Breath, and Foetus Art Terrorism?
6. Who sang thc theme tune from the movie *Born Free*?

203

1. Who was billed at 16 as 'Manchester's answer to Brenda Lee'?
2. Who 'thanked heaven for leetle girls'?
3. Which guitar hero was called 'God' by his fans?
4. Who used Manet's *Déjeuner sur l'herbe* to promote his latest product?
5. What is the term for piano playing that features a hot rhythm based on eight-to-the-bar figures in the left hand?
6. Which soccer team had a hit with *Blue Is the Colour*?

53

1. Marc Bolan.
2. Ronnie Carroll.
3. The Grateful Dead.
4. Reggae.
5. *Sheila.*
6. *The Tube.*

128

1. James Brown.
2. Billy Cotton.
3. Bee Gees.
4. Shirley Bassey.
5. Clint Ruin (Jim Thirlwell).
6. Matt Monro.

203

1. Elkie Brookes.
2. Maurice Chevalier.
3. Eric Clapton.
4. Malcolm McLaren.
5. Boogie (or boogie-woogie).
6. Chelsea.

54

1. Which bandleader was 'Mr Slow-slow-quick-quick-slow'?
2. Who had hits with *Perfidia* and *Walk Don't Run*?
3. Which US urban guerrilla group got its name from a line from Bob Dylan's *Subterranean Homesick Blues*?
4. To whom did Prince dedicate his first album?
5. Who went to jail for tax evasion in 1978?
6. Which TV series about a women's rock band starred Julie Covington and Rula Lenska?

129

1. Who was the man with the twangy guitar?
2. Who was backed by the Blue Caps?
3. Who invited the Beatles to breakfast?
4. Name Madonna's chart-topping album of 1986.
5. Who described the UN as 'run by thugs or representatives of thugs'?
6. Who wrote scores for 'Blaxploitation' movies such as *Super Fly*?

204

1. Who did the *Sun* newspaper call 'Pop's Mr Clean'?
2. Who sang about *True Love Ways*?
3. Who replaced Eric Clapton in the Yardbirds?
4. Which tax fugitive left England to set up a drum school in an Italian village?
5. Who scored the first international reggae hit with *Israelites* in 1968?
6. Who summed up their story in the film *The Kids Are Alright*?

54

1. Victor Sylvester.
2. The Ventures.
3. The Weathermen (later changed to Weatherpersons – 'You don't need a weatherman to know which way the wind blows').
4. God.
5. Chuck Berry.
6. *Rock Follies*.

129

1. Duane Eddy.
2. Gene Vincent.
3. Harold Wilson.
4. *True Blue*.
5. Bob Geldof.
6. Isaac Hayes.

204

1. Nik Kershaw.
2. Buddy Holly.
3. Jeff Beck.
4. Ginger Baker.
5. Desmond Dekker.
6. The Who.

55

1. What was Johnny Rotten's real name?
2. Which British Elvis imitator made it as a comedy actor?
3. Who wrote *Spanish Harlem* for Ben E King?
4. Which band is fronted by Bernard Albrecht?
5. What international incident caused The Ramones to regret releasing *Bonjo Goes to Bitburg*, an uncomplimentary song about Ronald Reagan?
6. Who wrote *Jesus Christ, Superstar*?

130

1. Who was known as 'The Father of Country Music'?
2. *Tutti Frutti* and *Good Golly Miss Molly* were written by whom?
3. What Beatles venture started as a boutique in Baker Street?
4. Who has an album out called *Talking with the Taxman about Poetry*?
5. What country does King Sunny Ade come from?
6. Which former star of the sixties has scored a hit with the TV series *Blind Date*?

205

1. Which US DJ was known as 'The Geator with the Heator'?
2. Who had a monster hit with a Hawaiian-guitars instrumental called *Sleepwalk*?
3. Who first got into the top ten in 1966 with *Sha La La La Lee*?
4. Who went from rat to saint in 1985?
5. What does RPM stand for?
6. Who co-presented *Six-Five Special* with Pete Murray?

55

1. John Lydon.
2. Jim Dale.
3. Phil Spector.
4. New Order.
5. The bombing of Libya. For some reason this act improved Reagan's standing in their eyes.
6. Andrew Lloyd Webber and Tim Rice.

130

1. Jimmy Rodgers.
2. Little Richard.
3. Apple (their record label).
4. Billy Bragg.
5. Nigeria.
6. Cilla Black.

205

1. Jerry Blavatt.
2. Santo and Johnny.
3. The Small Faces.
4. Bob Geldof.
5. Revolutions per minute.
6. Josephine Douglas.

56

1. Which pop star's brother told the press he was on heroin?
2. Who was backed by a six-piece band called the Twitty Birds?
3. Who organized The Concert for Bangladesh?
4. Who was Britt Ekland married to before meeting Rod Stewart?
5. Who said 'If the Stones' lyrics made sense they wouldn't be any good'?
6. Who directed the rock movie *The Last Waltz*?

131

1. Who is known as 'The Silver Fox'?
2. Which fifties rockabilly was promoted as a full-blooded Cherokee Indian (in fact he was only a quarter)?
3. Which band sang about a dedicated follower of fashion?
4. What kind of music is played by El Gran Combo De Puerto Rico?
5. What does ELO stand for?
6. Which movie was based on the life of rock DJ Alan Freed?

206

1. What is Richard Penniman's stage alias?
2. Who was Britain's 'King of Skiffle'?
3. According to the Beach Boys, which state in the USA produces the best girls?
4. In Bob Dylan's *Subterranean Homesick Blues*, who is in the basement mixing up the medicine?
5. Who told Smokey Robinson 'You better shop around'?
6. Which country singer starred in the movie *9 to 5*?

56

1. Boy George.
2. Conway Twitty.
3. George Harrison.
4. Peter Sellers.
5. Truman Capote.
6. Martin Scorsese.

131

1. Charlie Rich.
2. Marvin Rainwater.
3. The Kinks.
4. Salsa.
5. Electric Light Orchestra.
6. *American Hot Wax*.

206

1. Little Richard.
2. Lonnie Donegan.
3. California.
4. Johnny.
5. His mother (in the song *Shop Around*).
6. Dolly Parton.

57

1. Which DJ is known as Cuddly Ken?
2. In which song does Elvis have 'a wishbone in my pocket, a rabbit's foot around my wrist'?
3. Who capped his performance of *Fire* by igniting his hair?
4. Who said 'The world dictates that heteros make love while gays have sex'?
5. What was Liberace's trademark?
6. Who worked on a musical adaptation of Orwell's *1984*, but was denied rights to the book by Orwell's widow?

132

1. Who has been called 'The fat white grub' and 'Porky'?
2. Who fronted the Imperials?
3. Who wrote *Everyone's Gone to the Moon* for Hedgehoppers Anonymous?
4. Which AC/DC stalwart choked on his own vomit after an all-night drinking binge?
5. Which politically outspoken musician has been arrested nearly 200 times in his native Nigeria?
6. Which 1985 cult movie has a soundtrack by Iggy Pop, the Plugz, and the Circle Jerks?

207

1. Born Manley Buchanan in Kingston, Jamaica, this former cabbie is a reggae superstar. Who is he?
2. Who had a band called the Frantic Five?
3. By recording versions of *Let It Be Me* and *Take a Message to Mary*, Bob Dylan paid tribute to who?
4. What band was Malcolm McLaren's follow-up to the Sex Pistols?
5. Who was voted country singer of the year by *Rolling Stone* magazine in 1980?
6. Which movie did Ozzie Osbourne of Black Sabbath watch eight times?

57

1. Kenny Everett.
2. *Big Hunk O' Love*.
3. Arthur Brown.
4. Boy George.
5. Candelabras.
6. David Bowie.

132

1. Gary Numan.
2. Little Anthony.
3. Jonathan King.
4. Bon Scot.
5. Fela Kuti.
6. *Repo Man*.

207

1. Big Youth.
2. Don Lang.
3. The Everly Brothers.
4. Bow Wow Wow.
5. George Jones.
6. *The Exorcist*.

58

1. Who was born with the names Brian Peter George St John de Baptiste de la Salle?
2. In which song does Buddy Holly sing about 'The dreams and wishes you wish, in the night when lights are low'?
3. Which composer worked with veteran Broadway lyricist Hal David to play a major role in sixties pop?
4. Who named themselves after Nazi military brothels and regrouped after their lead singer hanged himself?
5. What is the street term for ultra-loud portable stereo radio-cassette players?
6. In which film did Lulu play a cockney schoolgirl?

133

1. Harry Wayne Casey has made it as who?
2. Who wrote the all-time pop classic *Will You Still Love Me Tomorrow*?
3. Who spent the night of 29 June 1967 in Wormwood Scrubs?
4. Which six-foot model-turned-disco-singer started out as a cult artist in New York gay discos?
5. Is Lita Roza: a) an Italian red light district; b) a singer; c) a brand of wine?
6. Who was female presenter of BBC Radio's *Family Favourites*?

208

1. Who was known as 'The world's sexiest male', with mobs of middle-aged women throwing underwear on stage?
2. Which early British Elvis imitator committed suicide?
3. Which legendary promoter started by running San Francisco's Fillmore East & West?
4. Who recorded a pop version of *Mary Had a Little Lamb*?
5. Which pop star is a former teacher and athletics champion?
6. Which producer of schlock records wrote a novel, *Bible Two*, in 1982?

58

1. Brian Eno.
2. *Well All Right.*
3. Burt Bacharach.
4. Joy Division.
5. Ghettoblasters.
6. *To Sir, with Love.*

133

1. KC (and The Sunshine Band).
2. Carole King and Jerry Goffin.
3. Jagger, Richard, and Jones of the Rolling Stones.
4. Grace Jones.
5. b) singer.
6. Jean Metcalf.

208

1. Tom Jones.
2. Terry Dene.
3. Bill Graham.
4. Paul McCartney.
5. Sting.
6. Jonathan King.

59

1. Who is 'Ol' Blue Eyes'?
2. In what song does Little Richard promise 'We're gonna have some fun tonight!'?
3. Who played the *Star-Spangled Banner* at Woodstock?
4. Who became famous with a band called the Blockheads?
5. Who won the Eurovision Song Contest with *Boom Bang a Bang*?
6. Who wrote a book about the punk revolution called *The Boy Looked at Johnny*?

134

1. Which fifties star was called 'The Caruso of teen schmaltz'?
2. Who had a chart success with a version of Sidney Bechet's *Petit fleur*?
3. Name the original four members of The Who.
4. Who produced Bay City Rollers' *We Love You* as a joke, and it went to no. 1 in Japan?
5. Which country has Juju music?
6. What was the Chas and Dave jingle for Courage Beer ads that became a nationwide catchword?

209

1. Which raunchy crooner, cartoonist, and journalist is nicknamed 'Good-time George'?
2. Whose first record to enter the charts was *Banana Boat Song* in 1954?
3. In Bob Dylan's *Desolation Row*, who were 'fighting in the Captain's tower'?
4. Who is Britain's most popular black singing star?
5. Who produced *Imagine* for John Lennon?
6. Which New York City Rapmaster formed the Zulu Nation after seeing the film *Zulu*?

59

1. Frank Sinatra.
2. *Long Tall Sally*.
3. Jimi Hendrix.
4. Ian Dury.
5. Lulu.
6. Julie Burchill.

134

1. Paul Anka.
2. Chris Barber Band (featuring Monty Sunshine).
3. Pete Townshend, Keith Moon, Roger Daltry, and John Entwistle.
4. Nick Lowe.
5. Nigeria.
6. *Gertcha*.

209

1. George Melly.
2. Shirley Bassey.
3. Ezra Pound and T. S. Eliot.
4. Billy Ocean.
5. Phil Spector.
6. Afrika Bambaataa.

60

1. According to the Stones, who is 'a gas, gas, gas'?
2. Who wrote a musical tribute to Gene Vincent entitled *Sweet Gene Vincent*?
3. Who took legal action to dissolve the Beatles in 1970?
4. Who duets with Kate Bush on the hit single *Don't Give Up*?
5. When you *Catch a Falling Star*, where should you put it?
6. Who starred in TV's *The Partridge Family*, before turning into a teen idol?

135

1. Which 'old-fashioned girl' attempted a comeback as a disco star?
2. Who played bass in Buddy Holly's New Crickets in 1959?
3. Who married Veronica, lead singer of The Ronettes, in 1968?
4. Who fronted The Rumour?
5. Who wrote a song with the lines 'The King is dead but not forgotten, this is the story of Johnny Rotten'?
6. Who sang the title tune in the 1954 movie version of *There's no Business like Showbusiness*?

210

1. Which DJ is nicknamed 'The Kid'?
2. In which song did Paul Anka complain 'I'm so young and you're so old'?
3. Which London University graduate had a hit in 1962 with *Come Outside*?
4. What was Huey Lewis and the News' multiplatinum smash album of 1983?
5. Frank Sinatra topped the hit parade after 1960 only once, with which song?
6. Who wrote the screenplay for the movie *That'll Be the Day*?

60

1. *Jumping Jack Flash.*
2. Ian Dury.
3. Paul McCartney.
4. Peter Gabriel.
5. In your pocket.
6. David Cassidy.

135

1. Eartha Kitt.
2. Waylon Jennings.
3. Phil Spector.
4. Graham Parker.
5. Neil Young (in *Rust Never Sleeps*).
6. Ethel Merman.

210

1. David Jensen.
2. *Diana.*
3. Mike Sarne.
4. *Sports.*
5. *Strangers in the Night.*
6. Ray Connolly.

[illegible]1

1. Who is known as 'The Boss'?
2. Who composed *Sitting In the Balcony* for Eddie Cochran?
3. Who was lead singer with Manfred Mann?
4. Which English psychedelic rock band toured the US in 1973 with Stacia, a semi-nude dancer?
5. Which country star was kidnapped in 1978?
6. Which Beatles album was turned into a (dire) movie?

136

1. How many children did Elvis Presley sire?
2. Awopbopalubopawopbam – what?
3. For whom did Bob Dylan write *Sad-eyed Lady of the Lowlands*?
4. What was Barbra Streisand's first hit in 1974?
5. Who wrote *It's All Over Now*?
6. Who played the title role in Nic Roeg's *The Man who Fell to Earth*?

211

1. What is Val Doonican's trademark?
2. Who checked the time and it was *A Quarter to Three*?
3. Who made a comeback album entitled *Roots* in 1969?
4. Who had hits with *Metal Guru* and *Get It On*?
5. Which rock guitarist played with Miles Davis?
6. Which legendary folksinger was the subject of the 1976 movie *Bound for Glory*?

61

1. Bruce Springsteen.
2. John D. Loudermilk.
3. Paul Jones.
4. Hawkwind.
5. Tammy Wynnette.
6. *Sgt Pepper*.

136

1. One.
2. Boom.
3. Sara, his wife.
4. *The Way We Were*.
5. The Womacks.
6. David Bowie.

211

1. Cardigans (or rocking chairs).
2. Gary 'US' Bonds.
3. The Everly Brothers.
4. T. Rex.
5. John McLaughlin.
6. Woody Guthrie.

62

1. Which UK chart-topper was born in Lucknow, India?
2. Who led a band called the Tympany Five?
3. Who founded Blood, Sweat and Tears?
4. Who in 1986 hired members of the San Francisco 49ers football team to sing on his album?
5. What is a UB40?
6. Which movie features James Brown, Aretha Franklin, Ray Charles, and Cab Calloway?

137

1. Who is nicknamed 'The Georgia Peach'?
2. Who claimed he got his gammy leg fighting in Korea (in fact he fell off his motorbike)?
3. Which record company turned down the Beatles?
4. Which band is named after an assassinated US President and his brother?
5. What does R&B stand for?
6. Who made the movie *Reynaldo and Clara*?

212

1. Who was very attached to his Aunty Mimi?
2. Where did King Creole come from?
3. Who had an unexpected top-ten hit in the sixties with *Milord*?
4. What was the Sex Pistols' only movie?
5. Which city gave birth to hip-hop?
6. What type of music features in the movie *Babylon*?

62

1. Cliff Richard.
2. Louis Jourdan.
3. David Clayton Thomas and Al Kooper.
4. Huey Lewis.
5. Unemployment Benefit Form 40.
6. *The Blues Brothers.*

137

1. Little Richard.
2. Gene Vincent.
3. Decca.
4. The Dead Kennedys.
5. Rhythm and Blues.
6. Bob Dylan.

212

1. John Lennon.
2. New Orleans.
3. Edith Piaf.
4. *The Great Rock 'n' Roll Swindle.*
5. New York City.
6. Reggae.

63

1. What was Donovan's second name?
2. Who first managed Tommy Steele?
3. Who has been described as 'the last hippy out of captivity'?
4. Who sings about a *New York State of Mind*?
5. How did Ricky Nelson die?
6. Who starred in the film *I Gotta Horse*?

138

1. Who is Reg Dwight better known as?
2. What was Buddy Holly's trademark?
3. Which group had hits with *Gimme Some Lovin* and *I'm a Man*?
4. Who said about athlete Carl Lewis 'I had the haircut first'?
5. According to Barry Manilow, where is the hottest spot North of Havana?
6. Which pop star features in the movie *Desperately Seeking Susan*?

213

1. Who is Richard Starkey better known as?
2. What time did little Suzie wake up?
3. Who kept splitting his pants?
4. Dave Stewart and Annie Lennox are the brains behind which band?
5. Who sang along with Stan Getz on *The Girl From Ipanema*?
6. Who played opposite John Travolta in the movie *Grease*?

63

1. Leitch.
2. Larry Parnes.
3. Peter Frampton.
4. Billy Joel.
5. In a plane crash.
6. Billy Fury.

138

1. Elton John.
2. Thick horn-rimmed glasses.
3. Spenser Davis Group.
4. Grace Jones.
5. The Copacabana.
6. Madonna.

213

1. Ringo Starr.
2. Four o'clock.
3. P J Proby.
4. Eurythmics.
5. Astrud Gilberto.
6. Olivia Newton John.

64

1. Three artists surnamed Berry had UK hits in the sixties. Can you name them?
2. What did Connie Stevens ask Ed 'Kookie' Byrnes to lend her in 1960?
3. Who sang about a warm San Francisco night in 1968?
4. Who or what is Double Dutch?
5. What language is 'oobedoobedoobewah'?
6. What musical includes *Who Wants to be a Millionaire?* and *I love you Samantha*?

139

1. Who was into 'dwarns' and 'rans' and liked to give the impression he was a sorcerer's apprentice?
2. Who is 'built for speed, got everything that Uncle John needs'?
3. Who murdered the song *Somewhere* from *West Side Story* in 1964?
4. What hippy supergroup was labelled 'boring old farts' by the music press in the seventies?
5. Who was the creative genius behind Specialty Records?
6. What show was described by Lord Butler as giving a whole new meaning to the Christ story?

214

1. To whom is Annie Ross and Georgie Fame's album *In Hoagland* dedicated?
2. Why in 1958 couldn't the Poni-Tails have the man they loved?
3. Which band said they imagined themselves as characters in a Dickens novel?
4. Who had a much-publicized reunion at Wembley in 1982?
5. In which part of London is Abbey Road?
6. Who starred opposite Deborah Kerr in the film version of *The King and I*?

64

1. Chuck, Mike, and Dave (of Dave Berry and the Cruisers).
2. His comb (*Kookie Lend Me Your Comb*).
3. Eric Burdon (*San Franciscan Night*).
4. Formation skipping dancing.
5. *The Language of Love* (by John D. Loudermilk).
6. *High Society*.

139

1. Marc Bolan.
2. *Long Tall Sally*.
3. P J Proby.
4. Led Zeppelin.
5. Bumps Blackwell.
6. *Godspell*.

214

1. Hoagie Carmichael.
2. They were *Born too Late*.
3. The Kinks.
4. Simon and Garfunkel.
5. St John's Wood.
6. Yul Brynner.

65

1. Who was known in the fifties as the 'Prince of Wails'?
2. Who was the Drifters' legendary first lead singer?
3. *I'm Alive* was a no. 1 for which band in 1965?
4. What girl did Kenny Rogers meet in a bar in Toledo?
5. What Abba song contains the line 'Since many years I haven't seen a rifle in your hand'?
6. Art Garfunkel's 1979 *Bright Eyes* was the theme from what movie?

140

1. Who or what began life as the Chicago Transit Authority?
2. Who once said 'when you have rhythm you have it all over'?
3. Who replaced Paul Jones in Manfred Mann?
4. Who won the Eurovision song contest in 1981 with *Making Your Mind Up*?
5. Whose 'Worldwise Texas Tours' featured snakes, cattle, buffalos, and cacti?
6. What was the theme song for the BBC series about HMS Ark Royal?

215

1. Pop stars Andy, Deniece, Don, Maurice, and Danny all have the same surname. What is it?
2. In what song does Emile Ford sing 'I'll get you alone tonight, and baby you'll find you're messing with dynamite'?
3. What Bowie character is 'Stepping into space and floating in a most unusual way'?
4. Who rhymes 'Ich liebe dich' with 'rhythm stick'?
5. Who was the first Greek ever to top the pops?
6. Who sings, or rather recites, *Wandering Star* in the film *Paint Your Wagon*?

65

1. Johnnie Ray.
2. Clyde McPhatter.
3. The Hollies.
4. Lucille.
5. *Fernando* (their only mistake in English!)
6. *Watership Down.*

140

1. The band Chicago.
2. Elvis Presley.
3. Mike D'Abo.
4. Bucks Fizz.
5. ZZ Top.
6. *Sailing* (by Rod Stewart).

215

1. Williams.
2. *What Do You Wanna Make Those Eyes at Me For?*
3. Major Tom.
4. Ian Dury (on *Hit Me With Your Rhythm Stick*).
5. Demis Roussos.
6. Lee Marvin.

66

1. What is DJ David Hamilton's nickname?
2. Who had a US hit in 1961 with *Rama Lama Ding Dong*?
3. Which Beatle had his tonsils removed which started a world-wide vigil?
4. Who wrote *Glad to Be Gay*?
5. How do Barry Manilow fans pay homage at his concerts?
6. Which rock musical is based on Shakespeare's *Othello*?

141

1. Which pop star has played Che Guevara and Fletcher Christian?
2. Who urged *Get a Job* in 1958?
3. Which two old schoolfriends shot to the top with *World Without Love*?
4. Who described a speech by Geoffrey Howe as 'a lot of crap'?
5. Where did Petula Clark advise you to go when you are lonely?
6. Who hosted BBC Radio's *Saturday Club*?

216

1. Who was discovered by Adam Faith and performed in a clown suit?
2. Who doo-wopped *Blue Moon* to no. 1?
3. Which sixties hit band pretended to be British but came from San Antonio, Texas?
4. Who was the Frankie in the newspaper headline 'Frankie Goes to Hollywood'?
5. Who, according to Benny Hill, was the fastest milkman in the West?
6. Elmer Bernstein had a hit with the theme from which TV detective series starring John Cassavetes?

66

1. Diddy.
2. The Edsels.
3. Ringo.
4. Tom Robinson.
5. They light candles.
6. *Catch My Soul*.

141

1. David Essex.
2. The Silhouettes.
3. Peter and Gordon.
4. Bob Geldof.
5. *Downtown*.
6. Brian Mathew.

216

1. Leo Sayer.
2. The Marcels.
3. The Sir Douglas Quintet.
4. Frankie Vaughan.
5. Ernie.
6. *Johnny Staccato*.

67

1. Who was 'The forces favourite' with *We'll Meet Again*?
2. What was Bruce Chanel's one and only no. 1?
3. Who recorded a psychedelic album entitled *Surrealistic Pillow*?
4. *Soul Deep* by the Council Collective was released to support which cause?
5. What does MOR stand for?
6. Which movie was based on a tall-tale melody sung by Arlo Guthrie?

142

1. Who became 'King of Rude Boy Music' with *007-Shanty Town*?
2. What do love and marriage go together like?
3. Which band, formed in 1967 in Woodstock, New York, called it quits at a gala concert at San Francisco's Winterland in 1976?
4. Who fronted punk band the Voidoids?
5. Who said 'I was never interested in talking things out. Either you do or you don't'?
6. Whose stories included 'The General Erection', 'Partly Dave' and 'Last Will and Testicle'?

217

1. Who was Peter Noone better known as?
2. Who was the BBC's Mr Latin Rhythm, Britain's Samba king of the fifties?
3. Which band included Pigpen, a heavy drinker who died in 1973 of liver disease?
4. Holly Johnson found fame with who?
5. What is the term used to describe bribe money paid to DJs to plug certain records?
6. Who appeared singing *Lili Marlene* in Amos Poe's film *The Passenger*?

67

1. Vera Lynn.
2. *Hey Baby*.
3. Jefferson Airplane.
4. The 1984–5 miners' strike.
5. Middle of the Road.
6. *Alice's Restaurant*.

142

1. Desmond Dekker.
2. A horse and carriage (*Love and Marriage*).
3. The Band.
4. Richard Hell.
5. Bob Geldof.
6. John Lennon.

217

1. Herman (of Herman's Hermits).
2. Edmondo Ross.
3. The Grateful Dead.
4. Frankie Goes To Hollywood.
5. Payola.
6. Debbie Harry.

68

1. Which eighties megastar was once 'a fat little Cypriot boy who hated the way he looked'?
2. Who wrote and recorded the million-selling *It's Only Makebelieve*?
3. Who had no. 1 hits with *1–2–3* and *Like a Baby*?
4. Which leading New Romantics featured double drum-rhythms from Burundi and yodelling vocals?
5. Which Jamaican singer is the 'King of Rocksteady Music'?
6. Which record company was founded by Chris Blackwell?

143

1. Whose dad wrote a book on basketball?
2. Who shot his bass player in the chest?
3. Who became the 'Voice of Sixties Protest' with *We Shall Overcome*?
4. Who said 'It's difficult to know how much to send to Ethiopia when you're a millionaire'?
5. Who claimed 'Elvis died the day he went into the army'?
6. Who wrote an autobiography entitled *A View From a Broad*?

218

1. Which rock legend was killed on 29 October 1971 in a motorcycle accident in Macon, Georgia?
2. Who had hits in the fifties with *Yakety Yak* and *Charlie Brown*?
3. Who fronted his Magic Band?
4. Which Tartan-clad teen sensations took valium and had two members treated for overdoses in apparent suicide attempts?
5. What is AOR?
6. Who starred as Annie in the 1986 West End production of *Annie Get Your Gun*?

68

1. George Michael.
2. Conway Twitty.
3. Len Barry.
4. Adam and the Ants.
5. Alton Ellis.
6. Island.

143

1. Mick Jagger.
2. Jerry Lee Lewis.
3. Joan Baez.
4. Sting.
5. John Lennon.
6. Bette Midler.

218

1. Duane Allman.
2. The Coasters.
3. Captain Beefheart.
4. Bay City Rollers.
5. Adult Oriented Rock (or Album Oriented Radio).
6. Suzie Quatro.

69

1. Who are the Gibb brothers better known as?
2. Who wrote *Johnny B. Goode*?
3. Eddie Hendricks and David Ruffin were the inspiration behind which hit group?
4. Lemmy is leader of which band?
5. Who said about the EEC, 'this place needs a laxative'?
6. Who re-arranged the theme tune for *Crossroads*?

144

1. Who is the boss of Virgin Records?
2. 'See you later alligator'. What is the reply?
3. What was Billy J. Kramer's backing band?
4. What colour is the rain when Prince is around?
5. Which country star is Lorretta Lynn's younger sister?
6. Which film featured Little Richard and Eddie Cochran?

219

1. Which rock star dated California Governor Jerry Brown?
2. What disease caused Ray Charles to go blind?
3. Who got to no. 6 in the UK charts in 1967 with *See Emily Play*?
4. Who formed The Damned in 1976 and left to go solo in 1984?
5. Who lived in Graceland?
6. Who played Alias in the movie *Pat Garrett and Billy the Kid*?

69

1. Bee Gees.
2. Chuck Berry.
3. The Temptations.
4. Motorhead.
5. Bob Geldof.
6. Paul McCartney.

144

1. Richard Branson.
2. 'In a while crocodile'.
3. The Dakotas.
4. Purple.
5. Crystal Gayle.
6. *The Girl Can't Help It.*

219

1. Linda Ronstadt.
2. Glaucoma.
3. Pink Floyd.
4. Captain Sensible.
5. Elvis Presley.
6. Bob Dylan.

70

1. Who has been called 'The King of Wimp Rock'?
2. Which singing sisterhood told Frankie Vaughan '*You Gotta Have Money in the Bank, Frank*'?
3. Which ex-rockabilly had UK hits with *Dreamin'* and *You're Sixteen*?
4. Who teamed up with Georgie Fame to re-form the Blue Flames?
5. Which ex-member of the Shadows became a Jehovah's Witness in 1973?
6. Which musical includes the song *Climb Every Mountain*?

145

1. Who left as his legacy the rock classic *Shakin' All Over*?
2. Who had a UK chart-topper in 1958 with *Story of My Life*?
3. 'There she goes with her nose in the air'. Next line?
4. Who plays drums in the Police?
5. Which fifty-year-old Rolling Stone had a 13-year-old girl friend?
6. Who sings the signature tune of the TV sitcom *Dads' Army*?

220

1. Who has lost a son and a wife by drowning and another son and brother in car crashes?
2. Who sings about an 'itsy witsy teeny weeny yellow-polka-dot bikini'?
3. Who made a record – *Witches' Brew* – and was arrested for keeping a brothel in 1972?
4. In which song do you find the words 'Wassa madda you? Why you no respecta'?
5. How many gold discs did Elvis Presley receive?
6. Which TV western hero was sung about as 'brave, courageous and bold'?

70

1. Elvis Costello.
2. The Kaye Sisters.
3. Johnny Burnette.
4. Alan Price.
5. Hank Marvin.
6. *The Sound of Music*.

145

1. Johnny Kidd.
2. Michael Holliday.
3. 'Funny how love can be'.
4. Stuart Copeland.
5. Bill Wyman.
6. Bud Flanagan.

220

1. Jerry Lee Lewis.
2. Brian Hyland.
3. Janie Jones.
4. *Shaddup You Face*.
5. Thirty-eight.
6. Wyatt Earp.

71

1. What is Sade's second name?
2. Who threw his jewellery into the sea and vowed to quit his evil ways?
3. What was Charles Manson's favourite Beatles tune?
4. Which DJ had a marriage break up, got hooked on valium and called his autobiography *The Living Legend*?
5. What is the word for black American music sold into the white pop mainstream?
6. Who directed the movie *Sid and Nancy*?

146

1. Whose biography is called *Is That It?*?
2. Which of the Everlys had a nervous breakdown and attempted suicide in 1963?
3. Which archetypal sixties band called on its audience to 'Kick Out the Jams'?
4. What is Laser 558?
5. Who is the favourite singer of Fergie, Duchess of York?
6. Who turned down a part in the movie *The Colour Purple* because it was too black?

221

1. Who is Private Eye's answer to the Beatles, Stones etc.?
2. Who was born in Ferriday, Louisiana in 1935?
3. Which rock star's father was a Rear-Admiral in the US navy?
4. Which Radio One DJ invited listeners to send in reasons why women go to the toilet in pairs?
5. How did Brian Wilson of the Beach Boys die?
6. Who sang the theme song for the movie *Midnight Cowboy*?

71

1. Adu.
2. Little Richard.
3. *Helter Skelter*.
4. Tony Blackburn.
5. Crossover.
6. Alex Cox.

146

1. Bob Geldof.
2. Don.
3. MC5.
4. A pirate radio station.
5. Chris De Burgh.
6. Tina Turner.

221

1. Spiggy Topes (and the Turds).
2. Jerry Lee Lewis.
3. Jim Morrison.
4. Bruno Brookes.
5. Drowning.
6. Harry Nilsson.

72

1. Who is Auguste Darnell better known as?
2. Who coined the phrase 'rock and roll'?
3. Who had hits with *Massachusetts* and *I Gotta Get a Message to You*?
4. Which 1983 hit single outsold all others before it?
5. Who said 'What are the Beatles?'?
6. Which soap opera tops the pops as well as the TV ratings?

147

1. Who did Shane Fenton return to the charts as?
2. Who invented the Duck Walk?
3. Who was a cloakroom attendant at the Cavern Club in Liverpool before topping the charts?
4. Who topped the charts in 1979 with *I Don't Like Mondays*?
5. In which town is The Grand Ole Opry?
6. Who starred in the movie *The Harder They Come*?

222

1. Who was billed as France's answer to Elvis?
2. How many times did Elvis Presley play the UK?
3. Originally called Cass and the Casanovas, they claimed to be Liverpool's first beat group. Who were they?
4. Who were the first Western pop group to play in Peking?
5. What does EP stand for?
6. Which Pink Floyd album became the basis for a movie?

72

1. Kid Creole.
2. Alan Freed, DJ.
3. Bee Gees.
4. *Relax* by Frankie Goes To Hollywood.
5. Noel Coward.
6. *EastEnders*.

147

1. Alvin Stardust.
2. Chuck Berry.
3. Cilla Black.
4. Boomtown Rats.
5. Nashville, Tennessee.
6. Jimmy Cliff.

222

1. Johnny Halliday.
2. Never.
3. The Big Three.
4. Wham.
5. Extended Play.
6. *The Wall*.

73

1. Who was 'King of the Twist'?
2. Who were billed as Britain's answer to the Andrews Sisters?
3. Which sixties heroine went on to make a highly regarded album entitled *Broken English*?
4. Who taught design at Harvard before joining Talking Heads?
5. Who chanted *2–4–6–8 Motorway!*?
6. Who sang the title song for the movie *High School Confidential*?

148

1. Who is known as 'Lady Soul'?
2. Who was always *Walkin' to New Orleans*?
3. Who was Muhammed Ali's favourite singer?
4. Which US President paid tribute to Bruce Springsteen?
5. Which British comedian had a hit with *Don't Laugh at Me Cos I'm a Fool*?
6. In which movie is a fight played out to the sound of the Marvellettes singing *Please Mr Postman*?

223

1. Who or what was Wolfman Jack?
2. Who does Buddy Holly describe as 'Pretty, pretty, pretty, pretty'?
3. Who was the bespectacled lead guitarist with the Shadows?
4. Which Sex Pistols song went to no. 1 despite being banned by the BBC?
5. Which member of European royalty is a pop star?
6. Which bestselling novel and movie about New York gangs gets its title from a fifties hit by Dion DiMucci?

73

1. Chubby Checker.
2. The Beverley Sisters.
3. Marianne Faithfull.
4. Jerry Harrison.
5. The Tom Robinson Band.
6. Jerry Lee Lewis.

148

1. Aretha Franklin.
2. Fats Domino.
3. Sam Cooke.
4. Ronald Reagan.
5. Norman Wisdom.
6. *Mean Streets*.

223

1. A famous US DJ.
2. *Peggy Sue*.
3. Hank Marvin.
4. *Anarchy in the UK*.
5. Princess Stephanie of Monaco.
6. *The Wanderers* (by Richard Price).

74

1. Who were Con and Dec Cluskey better known as?
2. Who first joined forces in 1956 as The Quarrymen?
3. Who invented the Wall of Sound?
4. Who is 'Aylesbury's King of Rock'?
5. Which Greek star got hijacked and lost a little weight?
6. Who did David Soul play in *Starsky and Hutch*?

149

1. Who is Harry Webb better known as?
2. On which street is *Heartbreak Hotel*?
3. What was Janis Joplin's favourite drink?
4. Which group is named after a Moscow street gang?
5. In Bob Dylan's *All Along the Watchtower*, what did the joker say to the thief?
6. In which movie does Ricky Nelson play a gunslinger?

224

1. Who was born Brenda Mae Tarpley and known as Little Miss Dynamite?
2. Who is the oldest of the Everly Brothers?
3. Which band invented British folk rock?
4. Who has 'a voice full of yuppy angst and designer depression'?
5. Which rock superstar owns Watford FC?
6. What was the full original name of the BBC's *Whistle Test*?

74

1. The Bachelors.
2. Lennon and McCartney.
3. Phil Spector.
4. John Ottway.
5. Demis Roussos.
6. Starsky.

149

1. Cliff Richard.
2. Lonely Street.
3. Southern Comfort.
4. Sigue Sigue Sputnik.
5. 'There must be someway out of here'.
6. *Rio Bravo.*

224

1. Brenda Lee.
2. Don.
3. Fairport.
4. Phil Collins.
5. Elton John.
6. *The Old Grey Whistle Test.*

75

1. Who is 'The Coalminer's Daughter'?
2. Who wrote *Running Bear* for Johnny Preston?
3. Whose signature tune is *In the Midnight Hour*?
4. Who filed a 200-million-dollar lawsuit against their manager Robert Stigwood and then made up?
5. Who is backed by the Famous Flames?
6. On *Ready Steady Go* what was the maximum rating a record could be awarded?

150

1. Who is Kenny Everett's version of a punk rocker?
2. Who recorded the original 1964 hit *Chapel of Love*?
3. Which international hit for Procol Harum was based on Bach's religious music?
4. Who announced in 1973 following a 60-date tour that he would never again perform on stage?
5. What is the term used to describe the blending of country vocal styles and rock rhythms?
6. Who played the title role of *Ned Kelly* in a film directed by Tony Richardson?

225

1. Brian Carl and Dennis Wilson were better known as?
2. Who was the first black musician to sell more records to whites than blacks?
3. Who went to the top with *Green Green Grass of Home*?
4. Who came to fame in 1974 with *Kung Fu Fighting*?
5. Who was the first to reach the scene of the car crash that killed Eddie Cochran?
6. What was the Beatles' animated cartoon movie called?

75

1. Crystal Gayle.
2. The Big Bopper (JP Richardson).
3. Wilson Pickett.
4. The BeeGees.
5. James Brown.
6. Five.

150

1. Sid Snot.
2. The Dixie Cups.
3. *A Whiter Shade of Pale*.
4. David Bowie.
5. Country rock.
6. Mick Jagger.

225

1. The Beach Boys.
2. Chuck Berry.
3. Tom Jones.
4. Carl Douglas.
5. A young police officer called Dave Harman who became Dave Dee of Dave Dee, Dozy, Beeky, Mick and Titch.
6. *Yellow Submarine*.

FOR THE BEST IN PAPERBACKS, LOOK FOR THE 

In every corner of the world, on every subject under the sun, Penguin represents quality and variety – the very best in publishing today.

For complete information about books available from Penguin – including Pelicans, Puffins, Peregrines and Penguin Classics – and how to order them, write to us at the appropriate address below. Please note that for copyright reasons the selection of books varies from country to country.

In the United Kingdom: For a complete list of books available from Penguin in the U.K., please write to *Dept E.P., Penguin Books Ltd, Harmondsworth, Middlesex, UB7 0DA*

In the United States: For a complete list of books available from Penguin in the U.S., please write to *Dept BA, Penguin, 299 Murray Hill Parkway, East Rutherford, New Jersey 07073*

In Canada: For a complete list of books available from Penguin in Canada, please write to *Penguin Books Canada Ltd, 2801 John Street, Markham, Ontario L3R 1B4*

In Australia: For a complete list of books available from Penguin in Australia, please write to the *Marketing Department, Penguin Books Australia Ltd, P.O. Box 257, Ringwood, Victoria 3134*

In New Zealand: For a complete list of books available from Penguin in New Zealand, please write to the *Marketing Department, Penguin Books (NZ) Ltd, Private Bag, Takapuna, Auckland 9*

In India: For a complete list of books available from Penguin, please write to *Penguin Overseas Ltd, 706 Eros Apartments, 56 Nehru Place, New Delhi, 110019*

In Holland: For a complete list of books available from Penguin in Holland, please write to *Penguin Books Nederland B.V., Postbus 195, NL–1380AD Weesp, Netherlands*

In Germany: For a complete list of books available from Penguin, please write to *Penguin Books Ltd, Friedrichstrasse 10 – 12, D–6000 Frankfurt Main 1, Federal Republic of Germany*

In Spain: For a complete list of books available from Penguin in Spain, please write to *Longman Penguin España, Calle San Nicolas 15, E–28013 Madrid, Spain*

A CHOICE OF PENGUINS

The Book Quiz Book Joseph Connolly

Who was literature's performing flea . . .? Who wrote 'Live Now, Pay Later . . .'? Keats and Cartland, Balzac and Braine, Coleridge conundrums, Eliot enigmas, Tolstoy teasers . . . all in this brilliant quiz book. You will be on the shelf without it . . .

Voyage through the Antarctic Richard Adams and Ronald Lockley

Here is the true, authentic Antarctic of today, brought vividly to life by Richard Adams, author of *Watership Down*, and Ronald Lockley, the world-famous naturalist. 'A good adventure story, with a lot of information and a deal of enthusiasm for Antarctica and its animals' – *Nature*

Getting to Know the General Graham Greene

'In August 1981 my bag was packed for my fifth visit to Panama when the news came to me over the telephone of the death of General Omar Torrijos Herrera, my friend and host . . .' 'Vigorous, deeply felt, at times funny, and for Greene surprisingly frank' – *Sunday Times*

Television Today and Tomorrow: Wall to Wall Dallas?
Christopher Dunkley

Virtually every British home has a television, nearly half now have two sets or more, and we are promised that before the end of the century there will be a vast expansion of television delivered via cable and satellite. How did television come to be so central to our lives? Is British television really the best in the world, as politicians like to assert?

Arabian Sands Wilfred Thesiger

'In the tradition of Burton, Doughty, Lawrence, Philby and Thomas, it is, very likely, the book about Arabia to end all books about Arabia' – *Daily Telegraph*

When the Wind Blows Raymond Briggs

'A visual parable against nuclear war: all the more chilling for being in the form of a strip cartoon' – *Sunday Times*. 'The most eloquent anti-Bomb statement you are likely to read' – *Daily Mail*

A CHOICE OF PENGUINS

A Fortunate Grandchild 'Miss Read'

Grandma Read in Lewisham and Grandma Shafe in Walton on the Naze were totally different in appearance and outlook, but united in their affection for their grand-daughter – who grew up to become the much-loved and popular novelist.

The Ultimate Trivia Quiz Game Book Maureen and Alan Hiron

If you are immersed in trivia, addicted to quiz games, endlessly nosey, then this is the book for you: over 10,000 pieces of utterly dispensable information!

The Diary of Virginia Woolf
Five volumes, edited by Quentin Bell and Anne Olivier Bell

'As an account of the intellectual and cultural life of our century, Virginia Woolf's diaries are invaluable; as the record of one bruised and unquiet mind, they are unique' – Peter Ackroyd in the *Sunday Times*

Voices of the Old Sea Norman Lewis

'I will wager that *Voices of the Old Sea* will be a classic in the literature about Spain' – *Mail on Sunday*. 'Limpidly and lovingly Norman Lewis has caught the helpless, unwitting, often foolish, but always hopeful village in its dying summers, and saved the tragedy with sublime comedy' – *Observer*

The First World War A. J. P. Taylor

In this superb illustrated history, A. J. P. Taylor 'manages to say almost everything that is important for an understanding and, indeed, intellectual digestion of that vast event . . . A special text . . . a remarkable collection of photographs' – *Observer*

Ninety-Two Days Evelyn Waugh

With characteristic honesty, Evelyn Waugh here debunks the romantic notions attached to rough travelling: his journey in Guiana and Brazil is difficult, dangerous and extremely uncomfortable, and his account of it is witty and unquestionably compelling.

PENGUIN OMNIBUSES

Life with Jeeves P. G. Wodehouse

Containing *Right Ho, Jeeves*, *The Inimitable Jeeves* and *Very Good, Jeeves!*, this is a delicious collection of vintage Wodehouse in which the old master lures us, once again, into the evergreen world of Bertie Wooster, his terrifying Aunt Agatha, and, of course, the inimitable Jeeves.

Perfick! Perfick! H. E. Bates

The adventures of the irrepressible Larkin family, in four novels: *The Darling Buds of May*, *A Breath of French Air*, *When the Green Woods Laugh* and *Oh! To Be in England*.

The Best of Modern Humour Edited by Mordecai Richler

Packed between the covers of this book is the teeming genius of modern humour's foremost exponents from both sides of the Atlantic – and for every conceivable taste. Here is everyone from Tom Wolfe, S. J. Perelman, John Mortimer, Alan Coren, Woody Allen, John Berger and Fran Lebowitz to P. G. Wodehouse, James Thurber and Evelyn Waugh.

Enderby Anthony Burgess

'These three novels are the richest and most verbally dazzling comedies Burgess has written' – *Listener*. Containing the three volumes *Inside Enderby*, *Enderby Outside* and *The Clockwork Treatment*.

Vintage Thurber: Vol. One James Thurber

A selection of his best writings and drawings, this *grand-cru* volume includes *Let Your Mind Alone*, *My World and Welcome to It*, *Fables for Our Time*, *Famous Poems Illustrated*, *Men, Women and Dogs*, *The Beast in Me* and *Thurber Country* – as well as much, much more.

Vintage Thurber: Vol. Two James Thurber

'Without question America's foremost humorist' – *The Times Literary Supplement*. In this volume, where vintage piles upon vintage, are *The Middle-aged Man on the Flying Trapeze*, *The Last Flower*, *My Life and Hard Times*, *The Owl in the Attic*, *The Seal in the Bedroom* and *The Thurber Carnival*.